VAMPIRE'S GRAVE

"A RHODE ISLAND STORY"

By: Troy Lembicz

TABLE OF CONTENTS

CHAPTER 1

DO NOT GO TO THAT CEMETERY

"Do Not Go To That Cemetery! Do you hear me?

Do you understand? I am telling you right now! Your
best bet is to stay away! Do not even visit that church!"
That is what my dad told me when I was about fifteen
years old. I thought he had a grudge against someone
who went to that church. So I asked my dad, "Why?" He
continued to tell me that it was just in my best interest to
stay away from there. He also proceeded to tell me that
I may understand when I get a little bit older. I thought
that he was just being a bit extreme. However, he never
told me not to do anything unless there was a reason.
My dad was never like that.

It was now the year nineteen ninety three, I just
had my seventeenth birthday and the month was
October. It is safe to say that two years ago my dad told

me never to go to that cemetery. Needless-to-say I forgot, however, a slight memory would kick in from time to time.

It was after school, Warwick, Rhode Island, about five thirty at night, when I went to my favorite pizzeria called, Cosmic, and I ran into two of my friends. We greeted each other with a fist bump and a hug. "Troy!" They said." I replied, "Tom, Chris. How the hell are you?" They told me they were chill. The cashier asked, "May I take your order please?" I said, "I just want a small pepperoni pizza." My friends told her the same for them as well.

We got our food and sat in the dining area talking about the latest updates. Typical things, homework, teachers, girls, you all know, stuff. Then Tom asked me, "Hey Troy, ever go to the midnight movie mash at the Warwick Cinema?" I replied, "No I have not." He told me, "Well you should." It starts at eleven o' clock every Saturday. I told him that I would go and check it out. It was only Wednesday and we still had forever to go before the weekend.

The weekend came and we were hanging out at my house, in the basement, playing guitars, drums, and just drinking. We were having a great time as we waited to go to the show at the Warwick Cinema. When the hour came we were picked up by Mike for the show. I never met Mike, however, he was a very chill person. We had a fun ride to the show.

When we got to the show it was the usual, friends greeting friends, girls talking to girls, gossip abounded, a lot of popcorn, and we just chilled in the lobby awaiting the event. Tom asked me, "Ready man?" I told him, "Yes." The doors opened, we entered the cinema. The lights went out, people started to shout, I was questioning everything to myself.

All of a sudden people started to throw harmless items at the screen and made fun of the movie. Tom was sitting next to me. "Tom? Why are they doing this?" He replied, "It is all part of the show man. Have some fun." So I started to yell at the movie as well. I felt strange doing that but it was funny. The whole show was in this fashion. It is safe to tell you, it was different, and it was strangely fun as well.

Monday morning approached and I was entering school for the day's classes. I was approached by Tom asking me if I thought Saturday was fun. I told him it was different and I will go again. We fist bumped and he told me, "I'll be seeing you after." We departed and I made my way through the noisy crowd for my classes. The bell rang and I just went through my day.

Tom met up with me after school and as always we went to our favorite pizzeria for some sandwiches. As we ate we were just talking about the latest gossip and other updates. "Are you still going to the show this Saturday?" Asked Tom. I told him I was planning on it; however, we still had the long week ahead. He replied, "Yeah, don't remind me."

We finished the week and we were hanging out for the weekend. I was with Tom, Mike, Chris, and Lori. Lori was with Mike and that is how we met. Lori was very chill. No one was dating, we were all friends. I was told afterward that Lori and Mike pretty much grew up together. They were best friends. We all just drank and played our instruments. We had an interest in trying to form a heavy metal band. So as the saying goes, "Practice makes perfect." So Friday night ended up becoming a band session party night. We left my house before my parents got home and we went to Mike's house.

Mike's House was very neat. He had a really neat guitar and he started to play some riffs for us. Damn, he was good! I wanted him to be part of the band, however he told me he was already in one. That was a bummer. The night ended up becoming a sleepover as we crashed at Mike's place. At least we did not have to drive as we were drinking. Mike's parents were on a cruise, so there was nothing to worry about. We all had a great time and we were planning for the night at Warwick Cinema for the show.

Saturday night came and we were gearing up to go to the Warwick Cinema for the show. We squeezed into Mike's car and when we arrived for the show, we saw police officers, with someone pulled over. "Sucks to be them." Mike said. We all were in agreement and then we learned that they were being charged for drinking and driving. We scurried into the cinema because we were drinking. Mike only had two drinks, but it was enough, so we blended in with the crowd.

While we were waiting for the show everything was noisy as usual. We were just chilling and having a conversation within our click. Then I noticed a girl that I did not see the week before. She was talking with some girls, kind of boisterous, long black hair, leather jacket, jeans, definitely a heavy metal girl. She was pretty, however, I was not looking for dates. My goal at this time was just chilling.

As fate would have it, we were in the same line for some snacks, she turned around and bumped into me, spilling her popcorn. "Crap!" She yelled. I told her, let me buy you another batch. She told me,"Don't worry about it, it has butter, I am not too keen on butter. My name is Melissa by the way." I told her, "My name is Troy," shaking her hand. She looked at me and asked, "Come here a lot?" I said, "I just started, you?" She replied, "Once in a while. Not all the time." I said, "It was good meeting you." She said, "You will see me again." I smiled, and went back with my friends.

The show started and it was the same scene as the week before, a different movie, same tactics. It was like a great rotten tomatoes thing for a movie. It was funny though. It's like throwing eggs at bad actors. I saw Melissa and she was well into it. It's like she knew her lines. My friends and I heard her the most. Like I said before, she was boisterous.

After the show was over my friends and I were making our way out of the door and someone called me. I turned to see that Melissa was the one that called. I walked over to her and she said, "It was cool meeting you." I told her, "Same." Then she asked, "Have you ever been to Tommy's Bar And Grill, on Bald Hill Road?" I replied, "I heard of it, but I never ate there." She replied, "Well you should. Best Burgers in Rhode Island. Next Friday, I'll come and get you, where do you live?" I told her my address and gave her my phone number. I told her I would be happy to try the grill out.

As I got back with my friends to return home I was approached by Mike. Mike asked, "Dude, you just picked that girl up?" I said, "No, it's not like that." He said, "Sounds like it to me." I replied, "I am just going to try some bar and grill with her on Friday." Mike said, "Um. Okay. I got it. Sure." Needless-to say- Mike did not believe me. According to Mike, I picked up that girl.

As always, the school week went by like an eternity passed. I can tell you that it did not have anything to do with Melissa. This always happens to me when we get to fall, going into winter. I don't care for those seasons so time just dragged for me in these months.

Friday came along and my friends and I had a jam session. After it was over I had a phone call from Melissa asking me if I was still going. I told her yes. So she was on her way to get me. My friends bid me a great time. They really thought this was a date. I could not talk them out of that. So I just laughed it off with them.

Melissa pulled up in a smoking black corvette! All I could think of was, Damn! Cool Car! "Jump in!" She shouted. I jumped in the car and she peeled out heading off to Tommy's. She was a lead foot however, not too bad, but still enough to get pulled over if she got caught.

We arrived at the grill and placed our orders. We ordered the same thing. The hamburger deluxe, large fries, and a soda.

Melissa asked me, "How is the burger?"

I replied, "Oh my God! This is one awesome burger!"

"See? I told you it was the best burger. No one can beat this," she said.

I told her, " You were right about this. I will have to show my friends this grill as well."

After this Melissa asked me, " You want to have some fun?"

"Sure." I answered.

She continued to say. " We will go to Exeter and I will show you this cemetery. You may find it a bit peculiar."

I asked her, "Why would we go to a graveyard?"

She replied, "Just trust me on this, you will not regret it."

It was odd, however, I told her that I would go. I was interested as to why she would want to go to a graveyard and consider it fun. All I could do was think that this was odd. I did not feel like I was in danger, it was just odd. "Curiosity killed the cat," as the saying goes, so we jumped in her car and headed to the cemetery.

It was about ten o' clock at night when we pulled on to a long, dark, and dirt road. I saw a church, and at this time, it was boarded up. Melissa pulled into the parking lot and we sat in the car, by the brick wall, that leads into the cemetery. Melissa shut off the car and turned out the lights. Luckily, it was a full moon so we were able to see the graveyard.

The graveyard was not big, nor was it very small. I would estimate about, at this time, perhaps medium size, long grass, weeds, it was old. I learned that it was a historical cemetery. Melissa started to tell me some things about the cemetery.

Melissa started, "This is Vampire's Grave."

I asked, "Why is it called Vampire's Grave?"

Melissa replied, "There is a person buried here that was an accused vampire. It is said that she haunts this cemetery, and that is how it got its name."

I realized that this was the cemetery that my dad told me never to visit. I was creeped out by that in itself. By golly, I hope my dad does not find out that I am here. He will ground me for a month.

"My dad told me never to come here." I told Melissa.

Melissa replied, "That's typical. There are many adults that this place creeps out. The myth about this place is strong. This cemetery is not a joke. There are many tales among the people that almost prove this grave is haunted. Many can try to argue it away, but that just means they never came here often, or at all. Come here often, sooner or later, find out."

"Wow, that's creepy," I said to Melissa.

She said, "That's nothing, trust me."

I asked her, "Well, what is it we are looking for? Are we going into the graveyard?"

Melissa answered, "I have not worked up the guts to go in there at night. The day inside there is enough to give you the willies. Right now, I am just looking."

"What are we looking for? Are we going to see a stick fly?" I asked her.

Melissa said, "No, it's not like that. You are not going to see pigs fly, zombies coming up from the ground, skeleton's walking, forget the movies. No, she is a ghost, but she walks herself as a vampire. It is said that it's her way of getting revenge"

"Who is she?" I asked.

Melissa answered, "Her name is Tori Brown. She was nineteen years old when she died. See that crypt to the far right?"

I said, "Yes"

Melissa continued, "That is where they placed her body, first. It was January, eighteen ninety two. They thought she was dead, but the snow preserved her body heat. So when the townspeople had people dying left and right, they thought it to be Tori. The people demanded that her dad prove she was dead. Her own father brought her out of the crypt, cut out her heart, burned it, and then he really buried her. It is possible she may have even been killed by her own father."

I said to Melissa, "That is really far out, I mean scary, wow! Her own father?"

Melissa said, "The medical personnel were not as equipped back then. She could have really been in a coma and they thought her to be dead. Yes, my friend, it is said that she is ticked, and she has been ticked ever since."

I was stunned at all of this history. It did give you shivers down the spine. I proceeded to ask Melissa, "So what do we see here?"

Melissa answered, "Feel the atmosphere. That's the big one. However, you can hear dogs, at times, running through here, a strange orb light, if you see that, leave right away."

I asked, "Why?"

Melissa continued, "If one sees that orb it is Tori's warning to leave. It is said that she is in a sour mood and she does not want company. Sometimes, you will even see her."

I asked Melissa, "Have you ever seen her?"

"No, not yet anyways, I want to though, that would be neat." Melissa said.

Suddenly she jerked and said, "We have to leave!" I was alarmed, " Why?" She just said "trust me," started up the car, slowly backed up and we drove down the road. I looked in the rear view mirror. I was hoping to see a haunting, however, all I saw was a police officer pulling into the cemetery. I thought, wow, this girl must be psychic.

"Are you psychic?" I asked Melissa.

She looked at me and said, "Silly, no I'm not a psychic."

I asked her, "Then how did you know to leave?"

She answered me and said, "Just call that woman's intuition. State law says after ten o'clock at night there is a no no. There have been quite a few cases of vandalism there over the years."

I looked down, shaking my head with a smile, and told her, "Well damn, that was a good call. Let my dad find out I was there and I will be the next vampire killed by his dad." Melissa laughed and said, "That's a good one. Let's go somewhere else now." I know a place where we can drink in peace."

We pulled into a field and she stopped the car. I got out and grabbed some drinks. We sat on the hood of the car and we were drinking slowly. I asked if I could ask her a couple of questions about the graveyard. She told me I could.

"What about the dogs that you told me about? What is that history? I asked her.

Melissa continued," That half of a house we drove by was where a family lived in the early nineteen hundreds. It is said that their kids went to the cemetery and provoked Tori Brown. That same night, the house caught fire, and everyone was killed in the fire, including the dogs."

I said, "That is way far out, creepy. We need to show respect I guess.

Melissa replied, "That is your best bet going there. Just respect the place, leave if you must, don't provoke. Just be chill."

I told Melissa that I would do just that if I went back there. Melissa proceeded to say, "Hey, next weekend I am busy, however, we can go back to the graveyard the following weekend. We will get there at about nine this time. This way we can have a valid excuse for a cop, if one shows up. And that is if one shows up."

I told her that would be cool. I was interested to see if I could spot a haunting. She ended up driving me back home saying she had a good time. I told her the same. She pulled off to return home, I went into my house, went into my room,and pondered all that I learned that night. I even wondered if I would be able to sleep. The truth is, I was creeped out, and it followed me. I had the willies for the whole weekend.

My parents were sleeping, however, I was not worried because nothing had happened. It was a great night. I was only terrified that my dad would find out

what happened, because like it or not, I did go to that
cemetery.

CHAPTER 2

STRANGE THINGS HAPPEN AT TIMES

It was now Saturday, the day after I was chilling out with Melissa, that Tom came over to my house. Originally, it would have been Tom and Chris, however, I learned that Chis had to go somewhere with his dad. So Tom and I decided to get a pizza from our favorite pizzeria and watch a movie.

Tom asked me how the date went. I assured him that it was not a date, however, he did not believe me. That was okay as I understood what it looks like from his point of view. My friends forgot that I was not actually looking for dates. I was just chilling. We got our pizza and we rented a movie from Blockbuster Rentals. We picked some sort of action thriller to watch.

Tom asked me, " So where did you end up going last night?"

I answered, "We went to Tommy's Bar and Grill. What a burger, we have to go man."

Tom replied, "That would be cool. I'll try it. What about after?"

I told him, "We went to a cemetery after that."

Tom said with a puzzled look, "A cemetery? Why would you go to a cemetery?"

I told Tom. "It's not an ordinary cemetery I guess. Supposedly it's haunted. It's the cemetery in Exeter."

Tom said, "Yeah, you mean that cemetery where the witch is. I know what you're talking about. Didn't your dad tell you never to…."

I interrupted, "I know, I know, however, yeah, I went. I was just curious."

Tom said, "Hey man, nothing wrong with that. I have never been there before. I only heard of it. I just never really put much thought to it, really."

I told Tom, "It was enough to send shivers down your spine. I was told some history, it was scary, I have to admit, I am creeped out. I think I understand what my dad meant now. I am not sure."

Tom said, "Hey, we will round up the gang and all of us will go sometime, yes?"

I replied, "Sure we can, however, perhaps at some other time. I just need to digest what I learned. This creepiness follows you. It is very strange."

Tom said, "Hey, I understand. Well, let's just jam our guitars and chill right now, forget the whole thing, it's Saturday."

I smiled, "It sure is, yeah, to the basement. I need some music."

Tom and I went to play some music and we spent several hours on our guitars. Afterwards, Lori and Mike showed up to my house, walking down our basement. I had to tell them about Friday night as well. We did not end up going to the movie mash at the Warwick Cinema. We just chilled at my house for most of the night. We did go to Bicford's for dinner, returned to my house, and jammed the night quietly as my parents were home as well.

My dad did not mind my friends. He only minded it when the guitars were too loud. We kept things low and chill so as not to annoy him. Then as fate would have it, we talked about that cemetery, very quietly so my dad would not find out.

Mike asked, "Is it true man? That place is haunted?"

I responded, "I did not actually see anything. I was creeped out though, however, nothing happened."

Mike replied, "Well, that still does not mean it's not haunted. Damn, I want to see a ghost."

Lori agreed, " You know, so do I. I only heard of that place."

I replied, "I will go again, I am just trying to get over it as of right now."

Mike said, "Respectable dude, we will go at some other point. No need to be in a hurry."

I told my friends we would all go very soon. I asked them to just let me get rid of the willies first. They all respected my wishes and we just hung out until everyone returned home for the night. We had a chill night, everything was cool, just a quieter night for what we are used to. Perhaps, it was a well needed chill night.

It was the following day, Sunday, I asked my mom to borrow the car for some lunch and a stroll in a park. My mom agreed and gave me her keys. I told her the truth, I went to get lunch at a deli, a walk in the park, however, I made my way to the cemetery.

It was about two o' clock, daytime, when I pulled into Vampire's Grave parking lot. I got out of the car and walked into the cemetery. Melissa was right, the day was creepy enough, let alone enter at night. It was strange. She was right about the atmosphere as well. It is almost as if you could hear voices from the past as the events took place.

I walked over to the first crypt and stood there gazing at it. I reached out my hand and I touched the old wooden door that was apparently vandalized. I gazed into the hole of the wood and I saw the bed Tori would have been placed on. After this, I proceeded to try and find her headstone.

As fate would have it, I found her headstone. I stood there for about fifteen minutes gazing at it. Then I opened my mouth to talk. "Tori, what happened to you? I mean wow. I am just shocked, Tori. Were you a vampire? Or just a victim of circumstance? I do not believe in vampire's, Tori, if you do walk this yard, why?"

Suddenly I heard a sound, I jumped three feet, I am telling you right now, I heard a voice behind me saying, "I am perfectly okay right now, it is such a pretty day today." I turned to look and found nobody there. I was alone, in the quiet of the grave, startled, spooked, eyes wide open. I quickly scurried out of the cemetery, got in the car, started it up, and quietly drove down the road. My heart was pounding. "Was that Tori?" I thought to myself.

I returned home, gave my mom the keys to the car, went into my bedroom, and just lied in my bed. I was scared, very scared, never have I….

Knock, knock as someone knocked on my door causing me to jump. "Troy, are you okay?" asked my dad. "Dad, I am fine, just tired." My dad came into the room. "Hey, you have been quiet all weekend. Did your date turn out good?" I told my dad, "It was not a date. It was a chill night. Melissa is cool. Everything is fine." My dad asked, "Then why so quiet?" I responded, "I don't know, perhaps I am not happy about another week of school." My dad laughed, "Okay, I understand. Just keep your grades up okay?" "Okay dad." I replied.

Monday morning came and I was greeted by my friends. Tom and Chris were okay. Chris learned of the cemetery and he wanted to check it out as well. I have to tell you the pressure seemed to be on. I did not even go with Melissa a second time yet. I tried my best to keep them level headed about it.

As we were talking I was interrupted by another guy, a football player. His name was Dillian. "Troy, I have a score to settle with you boy!"

"Dillian?" I said.

"Yeah punk, it's me, after school, you should not be walking." Dillian retorted.

I said, "So it's that same grudge, huh? I never wanted your girlfriend."

Tom jumped in, "Dude why don't you just step off!"

Dillian retorted, "Shut up! Or you're next!"

Chris said, "Bug off!"

Then a teacher came along, "Boys, break it up!" Now!" Where do you all belong right now?" We all told her, "In class Mrs. Flax!. She said, "Well I suggest you all get to class before I send all of you to the principal." We all left and went to our classes. I did not need this. Here I am, spooked out, and now a football player wants to fight me for nothing. I only said, "hi" to his girlfriend. Nothing more, and nothing less.

The hour came and my next class was with Mrs. Flax. Oh brother, I can't wait. I entered her class and it is safe to tell you all that she was watching me like a hawk. I did not understand why. Dillian was starting with me. I didn't do anything.

"Troy." She said to me, "Do you find that window more interesting than what I am saying at this time?"

"No ma'am," I responded.

She asked me, "Is everything okay?"

I answered, "Yes ma'am, I guess I am just not with it today."

She asked, "Are you sick?"

I said, No, no ma'am. I am just not with it.

"I suggest you get with it and look at me while I teach. This will be on the test, young man." She replied.

I straightened out my posture and paid attention to the class the best I could. I was borderline a D grade so I had to do my best. My dad was not happy about this class. I had to try. School history was not my thing.

The torturous school day was over and I went to a donut shop for a coffee. Tom and Chris followed me. "Troy we are here, man." "Awesome." I said. We sat down and talked about the day. My friends were getting a grudge against Dillian. I told them to just calm down and try not to get involved. I was trying to deescalate the situation, not make it worse.

Tom nudged me, "So dude, we are going this Saturday to the graveyard right?"

I asked, "What about the movie mash?"

He replied, "Ghosts are more exciting, man. Let's have some fun."

I asked him, "Can we wait until I go with Melissa the second time before we go?"

He replied with a puzzled face, "Why? It's just a graveyard dude. We don't need her for a trip to a cemetery. Are you scared or something?"

I replied, "We just do not know what we can get into. We do not understand much of this. If something is there, what will we do?"

Tom retorted, " Ummm run maybe? Ever occur to you to just use those two legs?"

I took a deep breath and said "Okay, we will go this Saturday. Just don't tell Melissa, please."

Tom said, "Dude, we will not tell your girlfriend, man. Trust me." Giving me a fist bump.

I replied, "She is not my girlfriend dude. I was just chilling with her."

Tom retorted, "Yeah, sure man, you've been day dreaming about her since Saturday. I believe you."

I assured Tom, "Tom, I am creeped out by the cemetery, it's not Melissa."

Tom said, "Well, it's either Melissa or Tori that you're day dreaming about. I tend to believe it's the live one. You look pretty normal to me."

Saturday arrived and we were all at Mike's house this time. I was wondering what time we were going to the graveyard. I wanted to go soon, however, my friends had a different idea.

Tom said, "We are going at night bro."

I said, "Why night? We can see more in the day."

Mike replied, "Graves, ghosts and hauntings are best at night, man. We all know this. I want to get freaked out tonight."

I gulped. "We still do not know if anything is there. Nothing may happen. We don't know."

Mike said, "Well, we all know a witch is buried there, so that is a start."

I said, "She is not a witch, she is a vampire."

Mike asked, "The difference please?"

I just sat there petrified. I hoped my friends were not going to do anything stupid. They were hyper about this whole ordeal. Lori came over and we had the original crew. We waited until eight thirty at night and we left for the cemetery.

We pulled into the parking lot of the church and we all got out of the car, looking around, and we started to talk. My heart was racing. I almost crossed my fingers hoping everything would be okay.

Mike started, "So are we going in or what?"

Lori agrees, "Yeah."

I said, "Let's just chill here first. We do not want to provoke anything.

Mike replied, "Provoke what? Look around you man."

I said, "We just do not know if this is really haunted. We should just be respectful."

Mike said, "Dude, there are five of us, nothing in there, we have the upper hand. Stop being paranoid. Watch this."

Mike stormed into the cemetery, Lori and Chris followed behind him, Tom yelling, "Yeah! Come on, show yourself Tori! Come on you witch!"

My friends, I am telling you right now I was so paranoid, that if talking to the dead is a sin, I am guilty, because I immediately said, "Tori, if you really walk this yard, please forgive my friends. Right now they are hyper, crazy, stupid, they do not know what they are doing. Please, just be patient, I will try and get them out of here."

Then my friends looked at me and said, "Troy, get in here!"

I went into the cemetery. We made our way into the middle of it, looking around, my heart pounding, and we started to talk.

Chris said, "See, this isn't so bad, why are we paranoid? Nothing is here."

Tom agreed, "Yeah man, there is nothing to fear. This is just a graveyard."

My friends looked at me. I just looked at them and shrugged my shoulders saying, "I don't know."

Tom started to yell, "I want to see the witch!"

I said, "Tom, keep it down, we do not need the police to come.

Tom replied, "And what if they do? We are not doing anything. We are just standing here looking for a ghost. That is not illegal, man."

"I know, but you sound like you belong in an insane asylum, keep it down." I said.

Suddenly there was a sound. Wham! Something hit the crypt door very hard. We jumped three feet.

I asked, "Okay who threw a rock at the door."
Everyone was puzzled.

Mike said, Troy, you are looking straight at all of
us. No one threw a rock."

I asked, "Son of a gun, then what the hell was
that?"

Then Lori saw a light. She said, "Hey you all,
look at the church. People are in there."

I said, "That church was boarded up last time I
was here, that's impossible!"

Mike said, "Well, it's open for business now, look
at it."

I looked at the church and my jaws dropped wide
open. This could not be happening. This was
impossible! That church is closed and boarded up.
However, I saw people there having a service. I saw

candles, a pastor, suit and ties, I was weak in the legs. Then we all heard a sound. Wham!

All of my friends turned pale as a ghost. No one was saying anything at all. I suggested that we should leave and go to our pizzeria. My friends agreed and we scurried out of the cemetery, got in the car, and quietly drove off to the pizzeria.

When we arrived at the pizzeria we ordered a large pepperoni pizza and we split it. The reason we did that was, we were hungry, however, our appetite was shattered. I knew my friends were creeped out. All of them.

I started the conversation, "Well, I guess that something is there."

Mike said, "Dude, let's just change the subject. I don't want to be rude, we are all great friends, but this time, I admit, I am humbled."

Everyone agreed saying, "Yeah, agreed."

I pat Mike on the shoulder and gave him a fist bump. I said, "Hey man, chin up, we are safe, nothing happened. It's all good man."

Mike replied, "Thank you, man."

We proceed to talk about our usual things. We talked about the next band practice, school, teachers, and the regular stuff for the rest of the night. Then we went back to Mike's house for some drinks. The rest of the night was chill. We seemed to get over it very well. When the hour came, we returned home for some rest.

It was Sunday morning and I left my house to go and see Tom. He answered the door and I was horrified at what I saw.

"Dude, what happened to your face?" I asked.

Tom said. "It was all scratched up when I woke up this morning."

Then his nose started to bleed. I gulped, my heart was pounding. I said, "Let's get you to a Doctor, man, please."

Tom said, "No, I'll be okay. I wonder if I fell out of my bed."

I said, "Tom, those scratches are not because you fell out of that bed. You don't even have a cat."

Tom said, "Well, I don't want to see a Doctor. I'll be okay, trust me."

I told him, "Tom, I think it's the cemetery that did this to you. We should just stay away now.

Tom looked at me, pointing his finger and said, "No, you hear me now, we are going back. We all agreed on this. All of us, as soon as I am better. And if you are too chicken, then, we are going without you."

Tom continued, "You go with Melissa this weekend. See your girlfriend, man. Learn whatever you can. I will not tell her we went. I swear. But after you go with her this weekend, we are all going again."

I was shocked at the pure obsession that my friends seemed to have developed over this haunting. Here is my friend, scratched face, bloody nose, no explanation, and he wants to go back. Even though I wanted to stay away for the time being, the weekend was coming and I still had to go with Melissa. I just thought to myself, perhaps I should have just listened to my dad.

I said to Tom, "I'll see you at school tomorrow?"

Tom replied, "No, I am going to tell my mom that I am not feeling well. I am going to heal a little bit first. I don't want to go with this scratched face.

I told Tom that I understood. We fist bumped each other and I returned home for the rest of the day. I went into my room, closed the door, laid in my bed, and just pondered the events. Eventually, I was able to fall asleep and I slept for the night. Monday morning approached and I went to school.

It was just a regular week at school with your normal day to day activities. I went through the week very quietly, thinking, withdrawn, and just kept to myself. I did not want to sound crazy in front of the other teens.

Thursday approached and something interesting happened. I overheard two teens, a boy and girl, talking about a cemetery. I walked over to them to inquire if it was the same one my friends and I went to. They told me it was Vampire's Grave. I gulped, 'you too?" I asked them.

"Yes," they said.

I asked them, "Did you all, by any chance, see anything while you were there?"

They told me, "We did not see anything, however, we heard very creepy sounds, like they were voices talking to each other."

I thought, "Whoa!"

They continued to say" One voice sounded like a girl asking her dad why he cut out her heart. We were petrified and we left."

I told them, "Thank you. That tells me that I may not be going crazy after all."

They asked me, "You see anything?"

I replied, "Yes, it was something and I just wanted to leave. I was not sure if I was just losing my mind."

They said, "Well, we heard voices, so you may have seen something. Maybe we all should just stay away."

I highly agreed with them, however, I still had to go with Melissa. So I just waited for an eternity for the weekend to come so I could go with Melissa. I did not want to go to the cemetery. It was nothing against Melissa. It was just the cemetery. I was still looking forward to chilling with Melissa.

Friday night finally came and Melissa pulled up to my house in her smoking corvette. I went outside to greet her and asked her to come inside my house for the moment. She agreed and we entered my house, went to the kitchen, grabbed a coke, and we talked.

I said, "Melissa, please do not be mad, I went to Vampire's Grave last weekend with my friends. I did not want to, but they put so much pressure on, that I agreed to go.

Melissa said, Silly, why would I be mad? You went to the cemetery, big deal."

I said, 'Well, that's great that you are not mad. I was trying to wait,but I…."

Melissa interrupted, "You don't need to explain. You can go to the cemetery anytime." Melissa was chuckling.

I continued, "My friends are having a hard time."

Melissa said with a pale look, "Oh no, did they get rude there?"

I said, "A little bit. I did not, but they were hyper, and got very stupid. I could not stop them. I did try to get them out as soon as possible. Melissa, I think there is something in there. I think it is really haunted."

Melissa said, "You think? That's what I was trying to tell you. It is haunted. I go often, only because I am trying to see if I can get a visual of Tori. We have to do it respectably though so as not to anger her. She is ticked off enough as it is. She is a very angry spirit."

I asked, "Is there a remedy for my friends?"

Melissa said, "Just stay away for the time being and it should pass. Listen, we do not have to go there this weekend. We can go to this smoking good restaurant that I know of in Cranston. It's about ten minutes from here."

I responded, "That's Cool. I hope this did not ruin your night."

Melissa said, "What! No way. I go to that cemetery when I go. It doesn't bother me. I just go when I go. We can go next weekend if you want."

I said, "Sure, next weekend. Can I still ask you some questions at dinner though?"

Melissa said, "Sure you can."

We left my house to go to Teddy's BBQ and Salad Bar on route one hundred seventeen, Cranston. As always Melissa peeled out speeding off. I was nervous when she did that. I just did not want to get pulled over by a police officer.

When we arrived at the restaurant it was jam packed. We had a ten minute wait, not too bad, then we were called to be seated. The waitress took our order and we were served a soda as well.

"So Melissa". I asked, "What is to become of my friends since the event took place."

Melissa said, "There is no way of telling for sure. However, I am confident that if they just stay away for the time being, everything will go back to normal. Tori is angry, but she does not hold a grudge against people forever. Tell them to be more respectful next time."

I said, "I just wished they would listen"

Melissa said, "Well, now that Tori got their attention, perhaps they will.

I asked, "Melissa, have you been haunted at the cemetery?"

Mellisa told me, "Me? Please. Many times. However, I practice what I preach. I just stay quiet, respectful, look around, and if I need to leave, I leave."

I said, "That is how I approached it last weekend, it's just my friends went wild. I can't control their actions."

Melissa replied, "No you can't. Since you did not do anything, I would think, you will be in the clear. I say, let's just hang out tonight, we will go next weekend to see if we can spot anything else."

I told Melissa, "Last weekend we saw people in the church having a service. That was impossible because we both know the church is boarded up."

Melissa replied, "Yes, it has been out of service for about eighty years to the best of anyone's knowledge. That church has been broken into many times, by cults, trying to speak with Tori."

I said, "That's too creepy!" I could never imagine trying to break into a church, that's haunted, to try and speak with a ghost. Damn, people are crazy!"

Melissa said, "Exactly. I could not imagine that either. I am just telling you about what I know of that church. It is what it is."

After we ate, Melissa and I returned to my house to hang out. Tom came over as well and he met Melissa that night. They shook hands, and they seemed very chill with each other. Tom was curious about some things as well.

Tom said, "Melissa, you gave Troy an earful about that cemetery."

Melissa told him, "I did, and I also heard what happened to you. Oh my god, look at your face. I feel so bad for you."

Tom asked, "My face is healing, but will this pass?"

Melissa said, "I will tell you the same thing I told Troy. Just stay away from there for now. Forget the place exists and it should pass. Tell the rest of your friends to be respectful next time. I blame myself for this."

I told Melissa, "No Melissa, don't blame yourself. It's my fault. I should have just listened to my dad in the first place."

Tom said, "No it's my fault! I should have never put the pressure on you Troy. I'm sorry, man."

I said, "Hey, it's okay man."

Melissa said, "Listen, we can do the blame game all night or we can have some fun and forget this. Let's go out for some drinks. Troy, we can go to that field."

I said, "That would be cool."

We all went to Melissa's car and she peeled out heading for the field. We dropped the topic of Vampire's Grave for the rest of the night. We drank very slowly and talked about many other things. That weekend turned out to be a great weekend after all. I am glad that I was paranoid for nothing.

When the school week arrived it was really cool to see Tom back. His face was back to normal. It looked like nothing ever happened to him. I was very glad to see Tom all better. I was able to concentrate more in my classes.

Lunch time came and Tom dropped in the cafeteria to see me. We fist bumped and hugged and the other teens said, "Welcome back Tom!" Tom smiled and said, "Thank you all."

Tom asked me, "Dude, are you still going to Vampire's Grave with Melissa this weekend?"

I told him, "Yeah, we are going there on Friday. After that she wants to go to the movie mash."

Tom said, "Sweet! I will be at the movie mash as well. Do me a favor bro."

I said, "Sure what is it?"

Tom replied, "After you go with Melissa to Vampire's Grave, Lori and I want to go after. We want you to come with us."

I asked Tom, "Tom, you and Lori are not going to do anything stupid are you?"

Tom answered, "No, not this time. That was really stupid of me. I do not want anything to happen to me again."

I said, "Then yeah, we will go. We should anyway before winter sets in. I will not be going there in the winter."

Tom replied, "Yeah, no kidding, and don't remind me about winter please."

I just laughed. We all hated winter. We just went through it and practiced our instruments during that season. We all did our best to stay occupied so that it would pass quickly. The movie mash would also be of help too. Plus, with Melissa's company to top it off, perhaps this winter will go by fast.

We all went through our school week and the weekend had circled back as always. Melissa picked me up, we went to Tommy's for a burger, then we headed off to Vampire's Grave. This time we talked about other things as well instead of just the cemetery.

Melissa asked, "So what is up with you and the band?"

I said, "It's all good I guess. We are not an official band. At least not yet. We are just practicing at this time. What school do you go to? You never told me yet."

Melissa replied, "I dropped out, however, I am going back. I should never have done that."

I asked, "Why did you quit?"

Melissa said, "Over a job. I loved having money and I did not want to give that up. I struggled with making money or staying in class."

I said, "That's understandable." I think I would be tempted to quit too."

She said, "Don't. It's not worth it. It gets boring fast. You don't go to school, but yet, your friends are all there. It's boring."

I asked her, "When are you returning?"

She replied, "I gave my two week notice. I am returning after that."

I asked, "Will you still have a job?"

Melissa replied, "During the summer. My parents were right. It's stupid to drop out. They told me to at least try and graduate high school."

I told Melissa, "Yeah, my dad told me the same thing."

As we were talking there was a very strange sound. I heard footsteps as if something was running. I gulped and I was terrified. Melissa looked pale too.

Melissa shouted, "Oh my god, it's the dogs!"

I asked, "Should we leave?"

Melissa said, "No, do not leave if it's just the dogs. That actually makes them angry. The legend says, they are friendly. It is their way of saying hi."

I said, "Wow! That is amazing!"

After this we heard and we felt a wind. The strange thing is, there was wind, but the trees and grass were not moving. I was scared. Melissa opened the window more and she listened. I listened too because she was listening. Then, as the wind was blowing, we could hear a very faint speech. If you listened close enough you could make out the words saying "Get out now."

Melissai looked at me with widened eyes. She said, "We have to go."

I agreed saying, "Yeah, I think you are right. Let's get out of here."

Melissa started up the car, slowly backed out and drove down the road. She started to tell me, "I saw the dogs before but the wind was the first."

My eyes were wide. I asked, "Did you hear that as well?"

She replied, "I sure did. It was time to go. That was very obvious."

I said, "I see that one hundred percent. Let's go to Cosmic and get some dessert."

Melissa agreed. We went to the pizzeria, we chilled there, with our dessert, and this time we talked about the experience. Both of us were laughing while we talked about it. I could not believe that I was laughing, yet I was.

Melissa said, "Oh my god! I can't believe that we saw that wind.

I said, "Me neither, but that wind talking was something else. I have never seen anything like that."

Melissa said, "Like I told you, that was a first for me. I have been there quite a few times, I never saw that."

I asked Melissa, "Have you ever seen the orb?"

Melissa replied, "Not as of yet. Tell me what you saw with the church last week, when you were with your friends."

I told Melissa, "Lori saw it first. Then Mike. It looked like people were in there, having a service of some sort. I even saw a pastor. No one looked at us. Do you know of any legend to that?"

Melissa said, "Only one thing comes to mind. I can not actually prove it, but I heard it said that Tori paints a picture of her funeral that took place in that church. You may have seen the funeral."

I said, "Damn, that is way far out creepy."

We were approached by a friendly lady that seemed to be in her sixties. She engaged in some small talk with us. She seemed very nice.

"Did I hear you talk about a certain cemetery?" She asked.

I said, "Yes Ma'am. You did.

She said, "I know all about the Tori Brown incident and that graveyard. Both of you have courage."

Melissa and I smiled. "You know about it too?" We asked.

She said, "I am friends with the family that are her descendants. Tori would be their great aunt if the events did not take place the way they did."

Melissa and I were shocked. "Wow!" Melissa asked her, "How did she pass away? I never knew the answer."

The lady said. "My name is Edna. She passed away from tuberculosis. It was a time when the plague broke out and a lot of people caught it. Unfortunately she did not make it."

Needless-to-say Melissa and I were addicted. Melissa proceeded, "So her dad did not accidently kill her?"

Edna replied, "I highly doubt it. Tuberculosis is very deadly. The Doctors did not know how to treat it back then. Now, we have medicine and vaccines for it."

I said, "This is wicked!" Edna smiled.

I asked Edna, "Ma'am, do you think the place is haunted?"

Edna replied, "Son, I have no doubt in my mind about that. I mean think about it, her life was cut short at nineteen years of age, she was accused of being a vampire, her dad cut out her heart. I think you would be mad as well.

Melissa and I laughed. "We sure would."

Edna continued, "I saw and heard many things at that grave yard. I go once a year to visit Tori's grave. Most of the time, I hear voices. Tori never bothers me. She knows I am friends with her distant family.

I was shocked. Then Edna said, "Look, you see that street over there? I live two houses down to the right, the white house. My husband passed away and I do not mind company. Drop in anytime if you want some history."

Melissa and I were shocked. "Thank you ma'am. We will take your offer and drop by."

Edna smiled and she left. Melissa and I looked at each other in amazement and we could not believe that this even happened. We would keep our promise and visit her. We went back to my house for the rest of the night. We hung out in my basement and I pulled out my chess game. We played chess and she won all the games.

Saturday night approached and we all went to the movie mash at the Warwick Cinema. Same old same old there with the usual crowd. We entered the cinema and we were approached by a girl named Dianna. She was a very chill person and it is safe to say we all hit it off well. She became friends with the whole crew very fast.

Dianna said, "Hey, I heard you all go to that haunted cemetery. I have never been there and I would like to see it as well."

Melissa replied, "We are all going next Friday."

I said, "Yeah, before the winter sets in"

Tom said, "Word on that."

Dianna asked, "So, have you seen anything in there?"

Tom replied, "Girl, let me tell you that I am still creeped out by what happened. I can still scarcely believe what happened to me.

Melissa said, "And this time you're going to behave, right?"

Tom replied, "Of course, mommy."

Melissa went to hit Tom and he ran. Melissa chased him in the lobby saying, "Come back here, wise guy!"

I was observing all of this, laughing my tail off. That was good. I did not expect the mommy line and it caught me off guard. The event was about to start, we all entered the theatre, grabbed our snacks and we were once again part of the show.

As always people were shouting at the movie, throwing harmless items at it. Dianna was laughing at all of this. She was having a good time. Then Dianna dropped her snack. "Damn it!" She said, I bought her another snack and we all had a good time yelling at the movie because it was so bad.

The movie ended and as we were leaving we were approached by a police officer.

He asked, "Do any of you know about vandals in a cemetery?"

I said, "No sir. I do not know of anything that may have happened."

The officer replied, "Well, I hear that your crew goes to a cemetery and I need some answers. Recognize this picture?"

I looked at the picture and told the officer, "I don't go to that one. The one I see is in Exeter."

The officer said, "Exeter huh? You're going to see that vampire-ghost aren't you?

I said to the officer, "Yeah, but we are respectful. We have not destroyed anything. We just sit in the car and watch. We are probably there for like thirty minutes, tops."

The officer looked at the picture, looked at me and my friends, and said, "Well, if you see anything like vandalism report it please. We are receiving complaints about vandals."

Melissa said, "Last time we were at Vampire's Grave the cemetery was in one piece."

I agreed, "It was. We never went in there."

The officer said, "Listen, it is obvious that the vandal I am looking for is in a different cemetery. This picture is not Exeter. Just report anything suspicious please."

We all said, "Absolutely sir."

The officer left and we were all relieved. I know that we did not do anything wrong. We just stood there, in the cemetery, and had the living wits scared out of us. Melissa and I never entered when we went, as it was night time. We all know this. However, we just did not want to be prime suspects number one either.

I asked, "So, are we still going this Friday, or do something else?"

Melissa said, "We are going, Just don't go inside. I don't at night anyway."

My friends agreed. "Yeah, we will not go in there. We will all stay in the lot and watch.

I said, "Okay. Agreed. We will just stay in the lot."

Dianna said, "I am a little disappointed, but I understand. We do not need to be accused of vandalism. We can go inside the cemetery another time, right?"

I said, "Yes."

Melissa said, "Dianna, don't worry, you do not need to be in the cemetery itself for anything to happen. Last time I went, we had a haunting just fine."

Dianna said, "Wicked cool!"

We all returned home for some rest. I went to my room, laid in my bed and just pondered everything that happened. I did not sleep that well Saturday night. It was a very light sleep and strange dreams. I gave up trying to sleep and I watched a comedy movie instead. After the movie I fell asleep okay.

The school week went by fairly quickly this time and I was looking forward to meeting up with the crew for the weekend. Before I went to see my friends, I decided that I would drop by Edna's house to say hi for about an hour. My friends and I were all meeting up around six o' clock so I had some time.

I knocked on Edna's door and she greeted me with a smile. "Hello young man."

I said, "Hi Edna. I just wanted to drop in and see you before I go out with my friends."

Edna asked, "Would you like a cup of coffee dear?"

I said, "Sure, thank you."

Edna asked me after getting me the coffee, "So, are you all planning on a trip to that cemetery?"

I said, "We are going tonight ma'am."

Edna said, "Let me just tell you this, be very careful."

I told Edna, "I plan on it."

Edna continued, "You do not understand. I know other people that had a strange fixation about the cemetery. It was so bad that they went out of their minds. I don't know if Tori was behind it, or if it was just their own minds in total obsession."

I told Edna, "Wow! Maybe we should take a break then?"

Edna said, "I would put it down for right now. The mental state of obsession can happen very quickly there for some reason. I know a man that was committed to the mental hospital because it was so bad. He is okay now-a-days. However, it still happened."

I told Edna, "That is scary. Yes ma'am, I think I will take a break after this trip."

Edna replied, "Yes, I would just bunker down for the winter. We might have a harsh one this year. My Farmers Almanac is telling me we may have a very cold winter this year."

I told Edna, "I will bunker down ma'am."

After the hour was over I bid Edna farewell and that I would visit her again. I left her house and my friends picked me up. We all went to Tommy's for the burgers and then we headed off to Vampire's Grave as we planned.

It was about eight thirty when we got there and we pulled out a drink. We all just stood in the parking lot this time. The incident with the police officer left us skeptical about entering and Melissa did not want to enter at night yet.

This time was different. It was a quiet night but the atmosphere was thick and very creepy. You could just feel it. I asked Melissa, "Is this the atmosphere that you spoke about the first time we came here?" Melissa replied, "It sure is."

All of my friends were creeped out as well. Even Dianna knew something was wrong. It did not feel right. It was like something or someone was watching you like a hawk. However, it was quiet and not one activity happened. We all decided to leave and we went to hang out at the field for the rest of the weekend.

I told my friends that I was going to take a break from the cemetery and bunker down for the winter. I told them they do what they do, however, I was going to take time off from going and just live in the reality that I am supposed to be in for now. My friends did not give me any grief. They actually agreed. They told me that they were all going to do the same. Melissa told me she was going to take a break as well. She said, "It may be exciting, however, there is no need to ask for anything stupid either." We all got her point. I mean after all, strange things happen at times.

CHAPTER 3

THE DANCER'S PLATFORM

It was now the year nineteen ninety four and winter had come to an end. The month was March and I was in school studying in the study hall. Melissa had approached me asking when I was planning to go back to Vampire's Grave. I told her probably when the weather warms up a little more. We also discussed if we were ready to even try to go back as we were taking a break.

Melissa asked me, "So Troy, how do you feel about everything?"

I told Melissa, "I am feeling a lot better. Much better than I ever have now."

Mellissa asked, "Should we return to the cemetery at some point? I am still trying to get a visual of Tori."

I answered, "Sure thing, I am only waiting for a nicer day. It has still been very cold out."

Melissa answered, "Agreed there. Yeah, I guess we will wait for a nicer day. Besides, I heard it said that spotting Tori is better in the middle and late spring months."

I asked, "Really?"

Melissa replied, "From my sources, it was told to me that late spring was her favorite season."

I said to Melissa, "We should go and speak with Edna about this history. See what she has to say."

Melissa said, "Hey that is a great idea. I would like to see her again anyways."

I said, "That would be cool."

After school was over Melissa came to my house right away. We walked over to Edna's house as it was not far from where I lived. We arrived and knocked on the door.

Edna opened the door and greeted us with a smile. She got some coffee for us and we sat down at her kitchen table. Edna was glad we stopped by.

"So my friends, What brings you here on this fine day?" Edna asked us.

Melissa said, "We are going to the cemetery again in late spring. Do you know any history about Tori's favorite season?"

Edna replied, "From what I was told, May was her favorite month. She just loved the outdoors during that time."

I said, "That is really cool. Is there anything we should watch out for at that time? You know, to respect the place and not anger her."

Edna said, "Aw, both of you are very nice. Just be respectful as you would go to any other cemetery, or place for that matter."

I told Edna, "I plan on it."

Edna told Melissa, "You need to be more careful as well my friend."

Melissa asked, "Why?"

Edna replied, "I can tell your fixation with that place is very high. I sense it because of what happened to my friend."

Melissa replied, "You can sense that?"

Edna said, "Absolutely. It was the same with my friend when he lost his mind. Remember, I told you that I visit the cemetery once a year?"

We both said, "Yes."

Edna continued. "There is a reason for that."

I said, "Wow! That is very interesting."

Edna continued, "Troy, you be more careful too. You are borderline."

I gulped. I was trying to be level headed and I did not see that I was borderline on the matter.

Edna said, "I can already sense the obsession starting with you as well."

Melissa asked, "Edna, Have you ever had a visual of Tori?"

Edna answered, "Many times. Like I told both of you, Tori does not bother me. She knows I am friends with the family. You can not force her out to get a visual. It must happen by sheer coincidence. That is where people get into trouble. They try to force the issue."

I said, "Miss Edna, you have so much knowledge on this. I am amazed."

Edna smiled and said, "I would just tone it down a little more if I were both of you. Have some teenage fun and stop thinking about a cemetery all the time."

Melissa and I laughed, "You know, you're right."

Edna smiled and when the hour was up, we bid her farewell, and we told her that we would return to see her again.

Melissa said, "I love talking to her."

I said, "Me too, She is very nice. So what are we going to do about the graveyard now?"

Melissa said, "I have an idea. We will go in May. After that we will take a break again. We should take Edna's advice. I think we are getting out of hand."

I told Melissa, "I think you are right. We don't need anything stupid to happen."

Melissa said, "No we don't. Now, let's get a pizza!"

I was all for that. We went to my favorite pizzeria and we got a large pizza and a coke. We split it and we just talked about regular teenage stuff. Then, taking Edna's advice, we went to Seekonk, Massachusetts for bumper cars. We decided to act like teenagers and forget the cemetery for a while.

The rest of the school year flew by and final exams were approaching in a hurry. The school was in busy mode knowing those days were on the way. The crew and I were itching for summer vacation so we could hang out and jam.

May finally arrived and as the weekend was coming I was approached by Tom and Dianna asking me when I plan to return to Vampire's Grave for a potential event. I told them that Melissa and I were planning a weekend very shortly. I also asked them how they were feeling from our long break.

Tom looked at me puzzled, "I am feeling great, why?"

I answered, "I just want to be sure. We do not need anything happening to us."

Dianna said, "Everything is cool here."

Tom said, "Hey man, the whole crew wants to go. All of us. We just want to see if we will spot anything."

I told Tom, "We will all go shortly. Be careful though, exams are coming fast."

Tom said, I know, man. Listen, I am planning on being chill like the last time. We all are."

I was relieved. I did understand the obsession level that Edna talked about. I sensed it within them too.

The problem was, try and explain that to them. I did not believe they would listen to me.

When the day finally came we all met up at Tom's house. We waited until eight thirty as usual and when the crew finally arrived we took our trip to the cemetery. We pulled into the parking lot, got out of the car, and just chilled.

Dianna started to walk into the cemetery. I was not expecting that. Mike followed, then Lori, Tom, Chris, and they said, "Troy, Melissa, come on."

They were all being polite and respectful. That was a relief. Melissa said, "What the heck." And she walked into the cemetery. I was shocked, then I followed. I had the creeps, however, I was glad that my friends were not doing anything wrong.

We were in the middle of the graveyard and we were all just talking and chilling out. All of us were watching for something. So far it was all quiet. Dianna was looking disappointed. I reminded everyone that we can not push the issue. All we can do is watch.

Then I started to think that it was going to be a quiet night and we should just leave. Mike said to wait just a little bit longer. We walked through the graveyard and we saw a path. We did not know where the path would lead. None of us entered the path at this hour. We all agreed to come during the day to check that out.

As fate would have it Dianna said, "Hey everyone. Look over there!"

We all turned and looked. We saw a light that looked like an orb. I asked, "What is that?"

Tom asked, "Think that may be a police officer?"

Melissa said, "No way! That is the orb! Look, it's getting bigger! We have to go! Tori is not in a good mood!"

After this we all heard the church bell starting to ring. Melissa said, "That is impossible! That bell has been dead for years and years! There is no way!"

As we were scurrying to leave the graveyard I saw another light. I waited until we were out of the cemetery, with the cars. I turned and I looked.

"Oh,my god!" I yelled. "Look at that, up at the tall monument stone, mid air!"

Everyone looked, Melissa's jaw dropped, everyone was pale, eyes were wide! Everyone said "What in the world!" We were all terrified!

What we saw was a female, in a Victorian dress, about nineteen years old, dancing on top of the monument. The female ghost opened her mouth and I saw the fangs as if she were a vampire. She looked straight at me. I was terrified.

I yelled, "Get the heck out of here! Run!"

Tom yelled, "Troy the cars are not even starting!"

I yelled, "What!? Then run! Everyone out. Run!"

We all ran an estimated mile up the dirt road, to a small hill, where we would chill out, and catch our breath. All of us were terrified, not knowing what to make of that. We were also worried about the cars because of the issue.

I asked, "So what do we do now?"

Melissa answered, "All we can do is wait. Let's chill out until this passes and we will try and get the cars."

I was terrified. "Get the cars?"

Tom said, "What else are we going to do? I agree, let's just wait."

We all nodded. None of us had a watch on so telling the time was not possible. We just chilled at that spot for an estimated hour and we talked about other things to try and clear our minds.

After the hour was up we started to walk, cautiously, to the cars, and we were crossing our fingers. The cemetery was quiet, everything ceased. We walked to the cars hoping for the best. The cars started up, we were relieved, we slowly backed up and left.

The next day was a day of great awkward silence. After the event took place, as we all hung out, nobody was really saying anything. Everyone was just shocked and it was hard to talk. I asked Melissa if we should talk to Edna about what happened. Melissa said she just wanted to forget the whole thing. She wanted no part of it.

"Are you okay Melissa?" I asked her.

Melissa replied, "Actually, I am not. I am so terrified I can not even concentrate on anything."

I said to everyone. "I think we have all seen her."

Everyone nodded. We were all still very pale. We tried to play some music but it did not work out on this day. We were all preoccupied.

I said to Melissa, "You got to see her. You should be happy because you got to see her."

Melissa responded. "I did, however, I am very frightened. I did not expect that at all. I never heard any background about the ghost dancing. That was so creepy, and I am so scared."

Melissa came over and gave me a hug. I held her as she started to cry. I felt so bad for her. I understood as I was shivering to my very core. I wanted to see Edna, however, I refrained due to Melissa.

I told everyone. "We should all take a break now." I think that we have arrived at the point where we could lose our minds."

Everyone nodded.

Then I asked, "Does anyone else agree that we should just try to forget last night?"

Again, they all nodded.

Then I said, "Okay. Let's all go to the field and have some drinks. We did not even touch them last night."

We all agreed and went to the cars. When we got to the field, we drank slowly, and we talked about other things. The hour came when it seemed that we were returning to normal.

A week has passed and I got a phone call from Dianna. She asked me to come over to her house. I agreed and went there right away. She looked very tired.

I asked Dianna, "Are you okay?"

Dianna replied, "No, I have not slept in days."

I asked, "Is it the visual that is giving you a hard time?"

Dianna nodded. I gave her a hug telling her everything would be alright.

Dianna said, "Dreams, I am haunted in my dreams. When I fall asleep I have a dream of the vampire dancing. I toss and I turn. I can not sleep at all. I am so wigged out it is not even funny."

I told Dianna, "Melissa was right. That cemetery is not a joke. I should have just listened to my dad. He told me never to go."

Dianna said, "When I went, I was only expecting creepy sounds or strange lights. I never dreamed of seeing a dancing vampire. I am so shaken up. I am sorry for sounding weird."

I said, "No Dianna, you are fine. You are not weird. I am still a bit shaken up too. I think this break will do the crew well."

Dianna said, "I want to see her again."

I said, "What? After all that happened?"

Dianna replied, "Not right away. At some point I want to."

I knew now exactly what Edna was talking about. The obsession level was building inside of Dianna. I could sense it. I tried to be level headed and reassured Dianna that a break was necessary for everyone. We will go again, However we needed to take a break. I invited Dianna to hang out with Melissa and I. I told her we should go to a restaurant and chill. We should talk about other things. Dianna said she would.

Dianna came to my house and we were waiting for Melissa. Tom also called me and said he was joining too. He also told me that our other friends were busy and they could not make it tonight. I told him I understood.

Everyone arrived and Melissa showed us her back. We were all shocked to see scratches on her.

"Melissa!" I shouted.

Melissa said, "I think it's from the bushes I ran into when we ran."

I told Melissa, "That is not from a bush, those cuts are too deep."

Melissa started to cry, "She hugged me and said, I've been having nightmares ever since the event. I am more scared than I ever was before."

I said, "Okay everyone, that's it. I am going to Edna's tomorrow and I am getting the scoop. This is serious. We can't have this. We have exams in two weeks. We need to study and pass."

Melissa said, I do not want to go and see Edna. However, I respect your wishes. Please find out what you can."

My other friends nodded and told me the same thing. I did not want to see Edna against their wishes, however, this was serious. It needed to be done. Exams right around the corner, and this is something we did not need.

It was now Sunday morning and I arrived at Edna's house. I told her everything that happened. I held nothing back. I did not care if she thought I was nuts.

Edna said, "Sounds to me that you all ruined your welcome for a little while."

I asked, "How so ma'am? We did not do anything wrong. We just stood there."

Edna said, "Tori is not one for company. Remember, she is angry. What you saw was called; The Dancer's Platform."

I asked, "Edna, is there a history lesson on that?"

Edna told me, "It is said that if one sees that, it is because Tori does not want the intruders to return. She tries to scare them so badly that they will never return."

All I could think was "Wow". I asked Edna, "What wrong have we done to anger her so badly?"

Edna replied, "Nothing dear. Remember, I told you that I visit Tori once a year. There is a reason I do that."

I said, "Wow, I guess you are right. Now to tell my friends about this."

Edna replied, "It is very wise of you all to take that break. If I were you I would wait months, if you ever return at all. It will pass."

I bid Edna farewell and I gave her a hug. I thanked her dearly for all the history she told me. I also told her that I would visit her again very soon. Edna smiled and wished me well.

I returned and I saw all of my friends. They were eager to learn what Edna had to say. I told them everything and I held nothing back. Now it was time for all of them to make a healthy decision.

I asked them, "We agree to stay away for a while now and return to normal?"

They nodded. I said, "Cool, we have exams coming up and we do not need any more things to happen. We need to pass our exams.

My friends agreed and we returned to our normal lives so we could study and pass our exams. We were all itching for summer break to come. We also started to make plans outside of the cemetery for summer activities. I am very glad that we all made a healthy choice. However, in the end of it all, I should have just listened to my dad.

CHAPTER 4

WHAT KIND OF SUMMER?

The summer finally arrived and it is great news that we all passed our classes. We were ready to go into our senior year so we could be done with school, get jobs, go to college, whatever plans we had. We have not put much thought to any of that yet. Not at this time to say the least.

We all took a break from going to Vampire's Grave, trying to forget what happened, live a regular summer, have some fun, however, some of us started to have slight temptations to return for another sighting. I was not tempted at all. I wanted a regular summer vacation.

At this time we were doing the usual summer things teens do. We were going to water parks, swimming pools, amusement parks, restaurants, among other things. My friends and I finally had a band formed and we played a couple of shows in Providence. The crowd seemed to like us. We also met some other bands too. That was very neat. Needless-to-say we were all having a great time.

One night came and Dianna showed up to hear the band practice. She liked the music very much. After practice was over she asked when we were returning to Vampire's Grave for another spook out.

I asked her, "Dianna, are you serious?"

Dianna said, "Yes, I want to see if I get another visual."

Tom replied, "In my book we are about due, man."

I thought to myself, "You gotta be kidding." Then I asked, "Haven't you all seen enough for the time being?"

Tom said, "Hey man, it's been a month."

I replied, "Yeah, and Edna said, months with an s after the word month."

Tom said, "I know. Hey everything passes right? We should be okay by now."

Dianna said, "Yeah, we will be fine."

I was shocked that they wanted to return so soon. The obsession was not at a healthy level in my opinion. I was still trying to talk them out of it but they would not listen. They told me either we all go, or they will go without me. I just sighed and said, "Okay, I will go as well."

I called Melissa to tell her the plans. Melissa said she was staying away for this time. She proceeded to say she was having a regular summer and she did not want anything to happen. I was sad about that, however, I understood. Melissa continued to say she will always chill with me and the crew. She was just not going to Vampire's Grave for a few months. To tell you the truth, I wanted Melissa's plan.

When I got back with my friends I was trying to reason with them. I personally wanted to wait until fall and have a regular summer like Melissa. I could not convince them.

I asked Tom, "Tom, then how about we wait for at least another three weeks and give things more time?"

Tom said, "Hey, that actually sounds pretty cool, man."

Dianna added, "I guess that is cool. Perhaps things will calm down. I just want to see her again. That was exciting!"

I said, "Yeah, too exciting"

Tom said, "We have not had this much excitement in our life. I never believed in ghosts until now."

I told them, "You two realize that we could just be asking for more trouble, right?

Tom replied, "That's what makes it so fun, man!"

Edna was definitely right about the fixation. The scary thought I had at this time was, "What if they are starting to lose their minds?" I wondered in silence if this was the first step. However, I was still trying to be level headed. Even though we agreed on three weeks, I tried to reason with them to wait longer. It did not work.

During the three weeks we were practicing with our band because we had a show coming up in Providence. That show was scheduled for two weeks and time was getting short. We spent that time jamming and we were not even thinking about Vampire's Grave.

The show turned out great and we met a few more heavy metal bands. We all had a lot of fun chilling out with them. We were starting to make plans to record our first demo and to tell you the truth, I hoped they forgot about the cemetery. They did not forget.

The third week arrived and we were waiting for the crew to arrive. Everyone arrived except Melissa as she was not going. Mike was startled that Melissa did not want to go. I told Mike that she was okay and that she just wanted a little more of a break. Mike was chill after learning the news.

We headed off to the cemetery about nine o' clock at night. When we arrived it was very quiet as one would imagine. There was a half moon on this night so we could see. We went to the headstone of Tori herself and we chilled there for about ten minutes. It was too quiet, except for the crickets, and other creatures one would expect. Once again. I started to think that nothing would happen at all.

After about fifteen minutes Chris saw the headstone and his face got pale as a ghost. "Hey everyone, look at this," he said.

We all looked at the headstone and we all had shiver chills go through all of us. I said, "This is impossible! There is no way!"

Mike said, "This is amazing, stone bleeds."

Everyone was paralyzed with fear. And then, as we were gazing at the blood, we started to see a face form. The face looked just like the girl that was dancing the last time we came here.

Dianna asked, "Is that really blood?"

I reached out and put my finger on the stone. My finger was wet, and it was red. My eyes were wide. Mike said as he was looking horrified, "Well, one thing is clear, it's not kool-aid."

I wiped my finger on my pants and my pants got blood all over them. It started to look like I got into a fight with someone. I wanted to leave immediately. Then we started to hear voices. The voices sounded like a teenage girl and a male adult.

The girl said, "Daddy, why did you cut out my heart?"

The male said, "The people demanded it. I never wanted to hurt you!"

My friends and I bolted out of there. We were so terrified that we ran past the cars and just ran as we did before. This time Mike yelled, "The heck with the cars! Later!"

We ran about a mile as before and we stopped at the same hill to rest.

I yelled, "This is wild! I mean look at my pants! This looks like I just killed somebody!"

Everyone was looking and they remained quiet, pale, speechless. Then we heard footsteps. We were all hearing this and our hearts went to our throats. I was afraid it would be a police officer. That would not be good. The way I looked with all of this blood, it was as if I killed someone, try explaining that.

Then to our relief it was some kind of animal. It looked at us, turned, and ran away from us. We were relieved. I wanted to go home, burn these pants, and just forget about this night. After about an hour we left, got in the cars, slowly backed up and drove down the road.

When we arrived at my house I was about to run into my house, to get rid of my pants before my parents saw me. Mike yelled, "Troy! Wait! Look!"

I looked at my pants and to my surprise they were clean as if nothing had happened at all! I almost fell down and fainted from fear! All of my friends were amazed and very pale. I returned to the car. We agreed to go and chill at the field for the rest of the night. As we chilled we never brought up the incident. We talked about other things to clear our minds.

It was Saturday and we were all planning to practice as a band so we could perform more shows. As I was waiting for the hour to arrive for practice, I had a phone call from Dianna.

She said, "Troy, Please come over!"

I told her I would right away. When I got to her house I was scared to see that her nose was bleeding very heavily. My heart pounded and I felt bad for her.

"Make it stop! Make it stop!" Dianna yelled.

I grabbed some paper towels and grabbed her nose in a first aid position. I said, "Dianna, we really need to stop going there now. This is becoming too much."

Dianna yelled, "No! I don't want to stop! I want to keep going! There is more to the story! I know there is!

I said, "Dianna, Listen to yourself. You are losing your mind. There is nothing more to the story. We know all that there is to know. The ground is just obviously cursed."

Dianna yelled, "No, No, No! There is more! I know there is!

I said, Dianna, get a hold of yourself please! Just look at you!"

I showed her a mirror as she was covered in her own blood. I said, "Dianna, do you want more of this? Because, this is exactly what will happen if we keep going!"

Dianna stopped and calmed down. She said, "I am so sorry,Troy."

I said, "Hey it's okay, Gather your thoughts. You stopped bleeding." I let her go.

Then I proceeded to say, "You need to get some rest. Take a nap. I will come and get you after. We are all just going to the field tonight. Nobody wants to go back to Vampire's Grave right now."

Dianna took my advice and she lied down. I reached down and I gave her a kiss on her cheek. I told her everything will be okay. She nodded and fell asleep.

As I was leaving her mom approached me. She started to tell me that she was very worried about her. She told me her behavior has been very weird as of late. Then her mom started to cry.

"I am so worried about her," she said

I replied, "I understand ma'am. I am worried too."

Her mom also said, "This really all started when her father, my husband, walked out on us. She has never been the same after that."

I replied, "I am so sorry ma'am."

She continued to say, "I am having her join counseling for now. I have been speaking with some of them, and they agreed to see her."

I said, "I really hope it helps ma'am. I really hate to see her like this."

Her mom replied, "Me too. Dianna said you and your crew are her best friends. She does not want to lose you all."

I told her, "Not happening ma'am. I really hope the counselor can help. I am in full support and I want her to get better."

Her mom hugged me saying, "Thank you very much. And from now on call me Shannon, please."

I said, "Okay ma'am, I mean Shannon. Listen, I told Dianna that I will meet up with her later. Right now she is taking a well needed nap."

Shannon bid me farewell and I left. I returned home as I was going to meet my other friends for a band session. As I was on my way I was thinking about the events that occurred. I was having a hard time getting all of these things out of my mind.

As I returned to my house Tom and Chris were already there. We fist bumped and they asked me how everyone was doing. I told them not so well at this point. I also told them that I will be taking a break from Vampire's Grave. Tom insisted that he would as well.

We grabbed our instruments and started to jam. Mellisa stopped by unexpectedly. I thought she was working, however, she had the day off. I was happy to see her and we told her all that happened. Melissa was heart broken that she was not there, however she assured us that she needed a break. We respected her wishes.

Melissa said, "We just need to get out more and do some fun things instead of just getting the creeps."

Tom said, "I agree that now is the time."

I asked, "Are you all going to change your mind like the last time?"

Tom replied, "No. Not this time. We really need to forget about this and just have a summer."

I said, "Yeah we do."

Melissa said, "Are we going to the field? I do not want to have a dead night because I have to go to work tomorrow."

I said, We are going tonight.

Chris asked, "Has anyone heard from Mike or Lori?"

I said, "Not yet. They are over due."

We all panicked and we rushed out of my house to go and see them. We were all very nervous that something bad happened to them. When we arrived we were all relieved that Mike was working on his car.

Mike said, "Damn starter! Hey everyone, do you think Tori has anything to do with this?"

I said, "Mike, it's a starter. This just may be coincidental."

Mike said, "Dude, this is the third starter. My car just keeps dying. I know it's the starter."

I said, "That's weird. Okay, I have an idea. Leave the car alone. Melissa, can you drive tonight? I want to see if the starter works tomorrow."

Melissa said, "Sure thing"

Mike said, "Thank you sis." Melissa laughed. Mike continued, "This is a great idea"

I said, "It's worth a shot."

To tell you the truth, I was glad that it was just a starter. With all that happened I had many other things go through my mind. This was basic at least, so it was a great relief.

When the hour arrived we left, got Dianna, and went to the field. It was fun to just act like teens, having some fun, and never thinking about a graveyard. We all got wild, drinking, chasing each other, beating each other, and being care free for once. I have to say that this ended up being a great night.

The next day came along and I discussed the issue about Mike's car with my dad, he told me, "Troy, it sounds like the alternator. If the car is dying on him, check that first." I said, "Okay dad."

I went to Mike's house and we checked out his alternator. Sure enough it was dead. Mike said, "Dude! Tell your dad I said thank you!" I told him I would. We fixed his car and it was as if nothing happened at all. I would have to say that this was probably not a haunting and what a relief that was.

One week had passed and all of my friends reported to me that they were beginning to have nightmares. I experienced a couple of bad dreams as well. What was very strange, the dreams were the same. All of us. That was impossible.

Everyone met me at my house. We were discussing the dreams and what this could possibly mean. All of us were just dumb founded and shaken up. All of the dreams were located in the cemetery.

Melissa was the first to ask, "Troy, should we visit Edna on this matter?"

I said, "We should, however, she will probably tell us to keep staying away."

Melissa said, "You're probably right."

Tom said, "Anyone think it may be Tori's way of asking us to come back?"

We looked at Tom with a crazy look. Melissa said, "Go back Tom? Really?"

Tom said, "Sounds crazy, but think about it. Maybe she just wants to have us over again."

Chris said, "Hey, I see it, That is possible."

I said, "No way, everyone. We are going to just ask for more trouble. We don't need any more trouble."

Melissa said, "No we don't."

I asked Melissa, "Melissa, you are having these dreams too, but you never went with us the last time we all did. What is going on with that?

Melissa answered, "I do not have any knowledge as to why. Perhaps, it is the fact that I was there all of the other times."

There was no way we were going to find out why this was happening. We all agreed to let more time pass to see if these dreams would go away. We ended up going to our favorite pizzeria and we went to a concert that night. We had a blast at the show. After the show was over we decided to crash at my place. This was an experiment to see if we would all have the same dreams.

As we were sleeping I sat up just to make sure everything was ok in the house. My parents were out like a light, the doors were locked, everything was normal. I returned to my room and lay down to get some sleep. I ended up having a dream. I saw a girl, in a Victorian dress, blonde hair, green eyes, look at me and whisper, "Troy, come visit me again, please." The words echoed in mystery, I woke up in a cold sweat.

I realized I was in my bed, I looked up being thankful. I checked on my friends and they were sleeping like bears. I was relieved, however, I could not fall back asleep. I just layed down and put on a comedy movie, turned the volume low, and watched it.

Morning came and everyone started to wake up. My parents did their usual thing, coffee, talk, and went to work. My friends woke up and they were okay. That was a relief. After we got our thoughts together we started to talk about the night. We were very curious about any mysterious dreams.

"Did anyone have any dreams?" I asked.

Everyone said they slept like bears. I told them all what happened to me. They were amazed about my dream. We tried to make sense of it.

Tom said, "Maybe we should go back. Perhaps it's an invite."

I said, "No way, Tom. This could be a trap for all I know."

Melissa agreed saying, "Troy is right. We need to just keep away. I am sure that this will pass. Remember that this is still fresh in our heads."

Chris said, "Maybe so, however, I see Tom's approach.

We all said, "Both you and Tom are crazy."

Melissa told Tom and Chris, jokingly, "You both should just become professional ghost hunters!"

We all laughed at that. Tom said, "Hey, why not? Sounds exciting."

We all said to Tom that he was just plain nuts and we grabbed our instruments to practice our songs. I had a show lined up for us in three weeks and we needed to practice. We put Vampire's Grave aside to concentrate on the upcoming show.

When the three weeks were up we had a great time at the show. Our band was next to the main one and the crowd was a very decent size. We were well liked by the crowd and we got to meet a few more bands as well. After the show was over my friends and I went to the field and we hung out until the morning pulling an all-nighter.

Summer was drawing near to its end and we needed to shift our focus for the senior year at school. We hated the fact that we had to return for the school year, however we were all eager to finish school and continue our lives. At this time we were all too busy to even think about Vampires Grave. We did not even think about it.

CHAPTER 5

HISTORY REPEATS ITSELF

The school year has now returned and we entered the doors for the first day. It is safe to say that my crew and I were not thrilled about our return, however, we were excited that this was the final year. As we met at our locker areas it was the usual, fist bumping, hugs, talks, gossip abounded, you all know, stuff.

My crew and I were pondering the summer that we had. Needless-to-say, we agreed that our summer was okay, but yet, not really that good either. Of course It was all due to the events. So we just put the matters behind us to think about the classes ahead.

After about fifteen minutes were passed I had another friendly encounter with Dillain again. I rolled my eyes and thought to myself, "This is going to be fun."

Dillain said, "Troy, punk, when I catch up with you…"

Tom interrupted, "Dude, just put it down, man!"

I asked Dillian, "Still the same grudge, Dillain?"

Dillain said, "Yeah, punk, what are you going to do about it?"

I said, "I told you before Dillain, I just said hi to your girl. I never wanted to date her."

Dillain replied, "Says you punk!"

I grabbed Melissa and said, "Dillain see? This is my girlfriend, right here!"

Melissa said, "Yeah, you jock! Let up!"

The principal came and yelled, "Break it up! All of you! Or detention on the first day back!"

We all dispersed and went to our classes. I thought to myself, "This is just fine. He still wants to fight me for nothing. What a year this may be." I did my best to stay level headed and try to diffuse the situation.

The first month has now passed and October was the month midnight movie mash would start back up on Saturday nights. I was wondering if we would even go to that. Sure enough, I got my answer.

Tom approached me asking, "Dude. Are we going to the movie mashes again?"

I said, "Sure. Anyone else coming too?"

Tom said, "I think everyone is in on it again. I know I will be going."

I said, "I will join you for those. I wonder if Melissa will join as well?"

Tom said, "No idea, man. Ask her."

I told Tom that I would ask her and we fist bumped to go to our class. When we were in between classes I ran into Melissa and asked her about the mash.

"Melissa, are you going to the movie mashes again? I asked.

Melissa answered, "Probably at times again. I don't go all the time."

I said, "I know, it's just that Tom wanted to know."

Melissa said, "Tell Tom what I said. I will be there, here and there. I just can't do those all the time."

I told Melissa, "It's all good. I will tell Tom."

I told Tom that Melissa would be going to the mashes. When we met after school to go to our favorite pizzeria, while we were eating, Tom asked me the big question.

"So Troy, when do you think we will go to that cemetery again?" Tom asked.

I asked Tom, "Again Tom? Seriously?"

Tom replied, "Sure, Halloween is going to approach, man. A haunting would be cool if we get one."

This sparked my interest. I agreed with Tom on my stupidity. I said, "Tom, you know, you're right."

Tom said, "Yeah, you see too, don't you?"

I told Tom, "We need to find out what the others think as well."

Tom said, "We should. Round up the crew, and for a creep out. It's Halloween."

When Friday night approached we met up at my house and discussed the idea for a trip to Vampire's Grave for a Halloween run. To my surprise the entire crew was hyper about the idea. We all seemed to forget about the past. Everyone was willing to return to test the waters once again.

Melissa said, "Yes! That would be sweet! Nothing like Halloween over there. I did that multiple times."

Dianna was thrilled. "I was waiting for another event there!"

Mike, Tom, Lori, and Chris all shared the same thing as we did. It is to anyone's wonder how we seemed to forget all that happened over a holiday thrill. I admit, I forgot as well.

The rest of Friday night was a jam session, a trip to the pizzeria, then off to the field for a hangout with drinks. As we were hanging out we were telling ghost stories just to hype us up. Needless-to-say teenage empty-headed-ness reigned supreme. For all we knew, what were we asking for?

Saturday night came and we went to the movie mash, Warwick Cinema for the opening event. It was noisy as usual upon entering those doors for the first time since last year. All of the sights were the same, typical, teenage, things one would expect. My crew just grabbed our snacks and we went in for the show.

The show had the same fashion as the year before. As always, it was like throwing rotten tomatoes at bad actors. I forgot how funny and ridiculous this was, however, that was the entertaining part. We all just chilled out and had a good time with the movie mash.

After the show was over the crew and I decided to chill at the field for a couple of hours. We were tired, however, we did not want to stop hanging out. I asked everyone to crash at my house for the night. They agreed so after the hours ended we went to my house for the night.

We got crazy in the basement with scary ghost stories again. I guess Halloween is getting to us. We were all having a great time and almost pulled an all-nighter. After this, we all slept for a couple of hours, hung out for a little while, then everyone returned home to prepare for the school week.

As we returned to school everything was normal as usual, with what you would expect. My crew was chilling out by the locker area and we were discussing plans for the return to Vampire's Grave. While we were talking, we were stopped by another crew, very cool teens, as they overheard us talking about the cemetery.

All of us engaged in conversation about the Vampire's Cemetery and we were informed that activity has been at an all-time-high. The crew proceeded to tell us that they have seen unusual things as well, and as we learned this, we were amazed. Melissa and I looked at each other wondering why this would be happening. Tom and Chris wanted to make this trip even more now as they learned of this as well.

The lunch hour approached and I was in the cafeteria having some french fries and then I was approached by someone else. I did not know who the student was, however, I have seen him before. I ended up learning why the haunted cemetery may have been more active at this time.

"Hi Troy. My name is Justin. I have some information that may be of interest to you," He said.

I asked, "Nice to meet you, Justin, what kind of information do you have?"

Justin told me, "I learned that Tori's main headstone has been stolen. I found it hard to believe, however, I saw the news on the matter."

I gulped, "Really?"

Justin told me more saying, "Yes, and I know the police are involved with the case. I saw that on the news as well."

I thanked Justin for telling me the information and I ran to see Melissa about the matter.

"Melissa! Melissa!" I yelled.

Melissa asked, "What's up?

I said, "Tori's headstone has been stolen. I just learned about this."

Melissa gasped, "NO!"

I said, "I learned this from someone named Justin. He told me it was on the news."

The crew caught up with us and we told all of them as well. Everyone gasped at this information. We were all quite upset as well. It is true that even though we never knew Tori, we thought, there is no reason for her headstone to be stolen. As strange at it seems, we ended up having a moment of silence for Tori.

After school was over, I left to go home, and as I was walking I saw a Police Detective at my school. I approached the officer asking him about the events that took place.

I said, "Hi Officer, my name is Troy. Can I ask you about the case of Tori's Headstone?"

The officer replied, "Hi Troy, I am Detective Barns, and yes, it is true that Tori's headstone is missing at this time."

I asked the officer, "Why would anyone do this?"

Detective Barns replied, "It's the lore of the stone. That is the reason. It's always the case when this happens."

I asked Officer Barns, "It's happened before?"

Detective Barns told me, "History repeats itself, Troy. This is definitely not the first time. For some reason when another group of teens come of age, someone tries it again."

I gasped, and then I asked, "Your team always finds it, right?"

The detective replied, "No, we don't have to. The vandal usually returns it."

I was shocked, "They do?"

Detective Barns said, "They do, they say the headstone is cursed. Something happens to the vandal and then they give it back."

I thanked Detective Barns for the information and I went to meet up with my friends. They were highly amazed about the information Detective Barns revealed to me. We all wondered if the vandal would return the headstone.

Two days have passed and the crew and I were chilling in my basement after school. I put the television on and we ended up watching the news. Sure enough, it was revealed that the vandal returned Tori's headstone to the cemetery. We all looked at each other in complete amazement.

I said, "The detective was right."

We all laughed, Melissa asked, "Should we even go there now? I mean, we do not need the police thinking we are disrespecting the place."

We all were wondering, I said, "Perhaps give it a couple of more weeks. We have time before Halloween approaches.

We all agreed. Even though we knew that we did not do anything wrong, we did not want the police to believe that we were. My friends and I never went there to do anything mischievous, we wanted to see a ghost. That was our sole reason for going. However, the police do not know this, technically speaking.

The following day I borrowed my mothers car and I took a trip to the cemetery by myself. Since it was daylight, I knew that I had a chance of being okay. I also brought a small guitar pick as a souvenir to place by the headstone.

As I was entering the cemetery I thought to myself, "I really should have just listened to my dad." I approached the headstone of Tori, which was now reinforced with a lockdown bar, and placed my guitar pick by the memorial.

I asked out loud, "Tori? What happened to you, that was so terrible, to cause these hauntings, make you so angry, and for people to come and take your memorial for themselves?"

I waited, then I said, "I do not believe in vampires, Tori. And I do not believe that you were a murderer either. What happened, Tori? What happened?"

As I was there I heard a voice behind me. I was chilled to the very bone. The voice said, "I am perfectly fine today. It is such a nice day."

I was scared and I slowly backed up, walked out of the cemetery, got in my mothers car, and I drove away. As I was driving I thought to myself, "Is that Tori telling me it is a nice day? I returned to my house and went into the basement. I picked up my guitar and practiced alone, pondering all that has happened to me the past year.

A couple of weeks had now passed and my friends and I were gearing up for a Pre-Halloween haunting at the cemetery. All of the crew rounded up, we went to our pizzeria, ate dinner, and drove off to Vampire's Grave wondering if we will get the creeps.

It was about eight thirty when we arrived at the cemetery. We got out of the cars and went into the yard. As we were walking, I was looking around, having visions from the past year, the church, the tall monument, which we called, "The Dancer's Platform," the headstone of Tori, and the events that took place. It is safe to say that all of this was creeping me out already.

As we were looking around we started to discuss the events that took place the past year. Needless-to-say, dumb idea as that was working our emotions up into a frenzy. I would estimate about twenty minutes passed and we were wondering if anything would happen.

I asked, "I wonder what will happen. It seems quiet tonight."

Melissa said, "It does, maybe we should just leave. This is not right, I can feel it."

Diana said, "You are right, something seems off."

Everyone was quiet, creeped out, chilled to the bone. We heard a sound from the crypt. It took place inside. We jumped, gasped, and took ten steps back. We heard a voice. "Let me out of here! Let me out of here!" We were pale, shivers took place, we darted and ran for the cars. The cars were not starting up. We proceeded to run like the last time and give it an hour. We went to the spot we discovered last year.

I asked, "Any history on this?"

Melissa said, "I do not know anything on this matter."

Everyone said the same thing. We were dumbfounded, catching our breath, calming down, and we sat on a rock that was there. As we were pondering, I said, "Well, I guess we had our Pre-Halloween event." Melissa slapped me. I laughed. It was a playful slap as I was being a wise guy.

After the hour passed we slowly walked to the cars and to our surprise, they started right up. It was the same as usual, we drove away, we were terrified, and we went to the field to hang out.

When we arrived at the field we were discussing what that was all about. It seemed that no one knew of any reason a voice would say "Let me out." I asked Melissa, "Should we see Edna?" Melissa did not want to. She really liked Edna, however, she did not want Edna to know that we were still visiting the cemetery.

When the night was over we all parted ways to return to our homes. We all hugged each other saying "See you tomorrow." I returned home and went to my room. I turned on the television, put on a comedy, and fell asleep.

Several days passed and I decided that I wanted to see if I could learn more about what happened. I decided that on Saturday, day time, I would see, if I could, by any chance, the property manager. I looked up the information. He had work hours every other Saturday from ten o' clock until noon.

When Saturday arrived I borrowed my mother's car and went to the office of the property manager. When I arrived I was shaken up about the events. I did not want him to think I was crazy. However, I decided that I would be honest with him at my risk of sounding crazy.

I entered the brick building that looked like it was built in the middle eighteen hundreds. When I arrived at the room, I gave a gentle, and a quiet knock on the door. The door opened and there was a man looking at me. He looked like he was in his forties. I gulped and he asked me, "Hi, what brings you here lad."

I said, "Hello sir, my name is Troy."

He said, "Hello Troy, my name is Rick. What can I do for you?"

He sat me down in the other chair of his office. I said, "I am here to get some information about the cemetery known as Vampire's Grave."

Rick said, "Ah yes, Vampire's Grave. We are having another round of teens just fixated with that yard again."

I asked, "Again?"

He said, "History repeats itself, lad. About every three to five years we get another batch of teenagers going in there to see a ghost. It always happens."

I said, "Sir, I am guilty of thinking it's haunted. I am very sorry. It's just that…"

Rick interrupted, "You and your friends developed a fixation there right?"

I said, "Yes."

Rick said, "Hey, it's ok." He smiled. "Let's take a trip to the cemetery right now. It's five minutes from here. I will explain to you what happened."

I agreed to go. We left in separate cars and we arrived there at about eleven o' clock. We walked into the cemetery and it felt different having the property manager with me. It was less creepy and I felt normal.

Rick said, "See that crypt?"

I said, "Yes, and that is where Tori was placed first right?"

Rick said "Yes, however, did you know that in the early nineteen hundreds a child was locked in there by a caretaker?"

I was creeped out. I said, "No, I did not."

Rick said, "The caretaker went crazy after working at this cemetery. It drove him out of his mind and he went to an insane asylum."

I gulped with fear. I wanted to leave right away, however, I stayed to be polite. I asked, "Did other caretakers take the job?"

Rick said, "Yes, however, only for a short time. Nobody seemed to last long working here. Now the State does not have the funding to care for this cemetery at this point in time. That is why it appears this way."

I asked Rick, "What about the legend of Tori Brown? What do you know about it?"

Rick answered, "It is all documented and you can get records from the Town Hall."

We started to walk toward the cars and he said, "See that rock? That is where her father burned her heart. He did that to prove she was dead. The townspeople here thought she was a vampire and killing all of the other people, when in fact, it was tuberculosis that broke out. The people did not know this, and back then, they did believe in vampires

I was chilled to the core of my very being. Then I asked Rick, "Do you think this grave is haunted?"

Rick told me, "Yes, but in a different way."

"A different way?" I asked, perplexed.

Rick continued to say, "Well, you see Troy, I do not believe in vampires or ghosts for that matter, however, the tragedy that happened here, is a haunting itself. If you really think about it, Tori's life was cut short, her own father had to cut out her heart, then bury his nineteen year old daughter, it's a sheer tragedy. Think about it. I believe that the people who visit here are having these experiences, because the tragedy itself starts playing with their minds."

I asked Rick,"So am I crazy?"

Rick answered, "I would not say you're crazy. I let people be their own judge of what they see here. Just because I believe a certain way, does not mean other people carry the same beliefs. After all, I cannot prove whether this graveyard is haunted or not."

We left the cemetery and I was bidding Rick farewell and thanked him for all of the information he gave me. I was especially wigged out learning that a kid was locked in a crypt by a crazy caretaker. All I could think of was, "That explains the voices the other night."

I decided that I was going to the Exeter Town Hall for the records that they had on the fearful graveyard. I was doing this without my friends having any knowledge of this. I did not want to go behind their back. I just wanted to learn what transpired, that was so terrible, this girl would stay so angry. Or I could have been losing my mind and I did not want my friends to lose their minds. I proceeded alone in the matters.

It was now Wednesday and Halloween was approaching in a few days. I journeyed to Exeter Town hall, after school, to see if I could get records. I approached the building as if it was built in the early nineteen hundreds. I asked the clerk if I could obtain the records for the incident about the Cemetery.

The clerk said, "I can give you copies of the records that are public, however, I can not give records about the classified things."

I said, "No, No ma'am, I just want the public records."

She said, "It will cost one dollar and fifty cents."

I said, "All good ma'am. I will pay."

As she was making the copies she asked, "So why do these records interest you?"

I replied, It's for a school report madam. We can choose a topic in our history class. I want to share Tori's story."

The clerk replied, "Well, history repeats itself I guess. You are the third boy that did a report on her in my forty years of being the clerk here."

I asked, "Third?" I was wondering if my friends came here as well.

The clerk responded, "Ten years ago I had another kid come here for a report. The other was twenty plus years ago."

That ruled out my friends. There was no way. I paid the clerk the money, bid her farewell, and returned home with the records. I took the records and put them in between my mattress so my friends would not see them. I was planning on sharing them with my friends. However, I wanted to see the records first, just in case, I was losing my mind. I returned to school and my friends. It was business as usual. We returned to life as usual for the time being and gave Vampire's Grave a break. We wanted to proceed with normal life affairs for the time being.

CHAPTER 6

LESSONS FROM THE PAST

It was Saturday morning and I decided to visit Edna as I have not seen her in a while. I knocked on her door and she answered me with a smile. It was great to see her again. This time, to my surprise she had company. I was not expecting the fact that it was one of her friends, Tori's distant relative. I almost fainted.

Edna said, "Troy, this is Kenny. He is one of the relatives of Tori."

I gasped, "It's nice to meet you sir." I was shaking his hand.

Kenny said, "Troy, it is a pleasure meeting you. Yes, Tori would have been my great aunt if the tragedy did not occur as it did."

I said, "This is truly wild. I am really talking with an actual relative. I was not expecting this."

Kenny laughed and said, "Edna tells me you have developed a fixation about the story. I would advise you to just keep a level head son. That graveyard has a tremendous effect on people.

I said, "Apparently so, sir. I guess I am starting to lose my mind."

Kenny said. "I would not say that yet. I do not believe you are at that point. I can sense the level of fascination though. I have seen it before with a few people I have met."

I figured this gentleman would know. I mean, after all, this was one of Tori's relatives. If anyone knows some things, this man is the one to talk to."

I asked Kenny, "Do you think the grave is haunted?"

Kenny laughed saying, "Son, let me tell you this. I have been on this earth for sixty one years. I have seen some things in my lifetime. We can't explain, nor can we understand, all that earth has to offer. However, I can tell you this, I have never seen a place, that I have been, that was so creepy as that cemetery. I can not prove if it is haunted or not. I can tell you that I have had my share of sightings there.

I gasped asking, "Have you seen Tori too?"

Kenny replied, "I am a relative of the family. What do you think?"

I said, "I think you have."

Kenny pointed his finger at me and winked saying, "Bingo."

I asked Kenny, "Kenny? What happened, that was so terrible, that made the grave haunted, and Tori to be so angry?"

Kenny replied, "The story itself. The most tragic thing, son, is that Tori's life was cut so short. Think about it, if you died right now you would probably be mad too. What would you have become if death never happened to you. That would be a mystery forever."

I said, "I understand sir. Wow, I never did before, but now, I think I understand."

Kenny replied, "Also, think about being accused of something you never done, or were, to top it all off."

I was awestruck. "Now I understand. Now, I believe I discovered the meaning of the haunted grave. I have never seen it like that before."

Kenny said, "Bingo again, son."

This time, I learned more than I could ever imagine. I saw this in a whole new light. I was thrilled, and yet, very amazed.

Edna got up and pulled out a box. She looked at Kenny and asked, "Should I Ken?" Ken nodded.

Edna pulled a necklace out of the box and put it around my neck. She said, "This was Tori's favorite necklace. I believe in my heart she would like you to have it." Kenny smiled as he was looking at me. I almost fell over.

I started to cry and I said, "I will never take this off."

Edna said, "Now dear, be reasonable, you do not want to choke while you are sleeping."

I said laughing, "You are probably right."

The three of us talked about a few more things for a couple of hours. Then I bid them farewell and I left to return to my house. I told Edna that I would visit again shortly and I told Kenny that I hoped to see him again.

I returned home and I went to my room and studied the records. Now that I spoke with Kenny, I believed that I would understand the records. When I pulled them out I read, as the media was in those days, titles, "The Dead Has Come Back To Life," "Ten People Dead In One Night," "Tori Is To Blame," "Girl Accused, She Is A Vampire," "Towns Folk Demand Answers."

I read all of the news articles. After that I pulled out another article that read, "Tori's Father To Prove Tori Is Dead." The last article that I had was, "Father Cut Out His Daughter's Heart, Towns People Are Safe Once Again." I read all of the articles with much care and interest. The meeting with Kenny sure helped me to understand what happened.

Now it was Saturday night and I decided to show my friends the articles. They were amazed to learn what I had and they were curious why I did this without their knowledge.

Tom asked, "Troy, how did you get these?"

I said, They are from the Town Hall. " They all cost one dollar and fifty cents, and anyone can get them."

Melissa said, "This is far out, wicked! This is actual history! I love it!"

Dianna replied, "You are so lucky."

I told them, "This is not luck, you can all get the records."

My friends laughed. Now the question was asked by Tom, "So Troy when are we going back? I want more hauntings."

I told them, "We go on Halloween"

Tom smiled, "Really?"

I said, "Yes, I want to go."

Melissa looked at me crazy, "Troy are you for real?"

I told them, "I am. Call me crazy, but I want to see something."

Tom said, "That's the spirit, man."

Dianna said, "Yeah."

I proceeded to tell them, "I have a theory. I want to see something."

Melissa asked, "See what?"

I said, "I do not think she is evil."

Tom looked at me crazy and said, "What dude?" Look what happened to us in the past. Tori is truly angry, dude, trust me, she's evil."

I knew my friends would not understand. After all, they were not at Edna's house when I learned the information that I had. So I understood from their point of view. I was not mad at them. However, they thought I did go crazy. We were still happy to go back to Vampire's Grave and they wanted a haunting.

Halloween arrived and we all geared up to go for a Vampire's Gave trip. As stated, my friends wanted a haunting, I was going there for a different reason. The only mystery that bothered me was, what am I looking for? I had to go to the cemetery and let the trip itself tell me.

We had some nerves as well. Going there on Halloween night? This was very creepy in itself. I do not know if other teens did that in the past, however, we were. Mike came over with Lori, we all got in the cars, and left for the cemetery.

When we arrived, we got out of the vehicles and as always, just looked around. This was very creepy as it was Halloween night. As we were chilling out we started to talk about my theory a little bit.

"Troy, Now you say that you do not believe this is evil?" Asked Tom.

I replied, "No, creepy yes, evil no."

Tom said, "Dude, feel the atmosphere, man. It's evil, bro."

I told my friends, "I understand where you are all coming from. However, I do not believe that Tori is evil. Angry, yes, evil no."

Melissa asked, "How do you even get this theory?"

I responded, "I do not know, except for the fact of the tragedy itself that took place here. In all honesty, I think Tori may be trying to tell us something. She always has been, for all this time. I think that no one was listening. I think that everyone who came here, getting these hauntings, believed it to be evil, and never gave it a second thought."

Tom replied, "Your crazy, man"

I replied, "I could be losing my mind. It's possible. Remember, this is just a theory. All I want to do is, see if this theory is correct."

As we were talking Lori spotted a sight that was taking place. I saw her eyes get very wide as she said, "Look over by the crypt." We all looked and our faces dropped pale. I was stunned, however, I was keeping a level head.

Everyone started to say, "Let's go, let's get out of here, come on."

I said, "Hold on, stay calm, defy your fears, I want to see this."

My friends looked at me crazy. They thought I lost my mind and that I became too fixated. What we saw was, as if it were a funeral, in front of the crypt. We saw spirits attending this funeral and then, to our horror, the ghosts turned their heads and looked at us.

I yelled, "I am not leaving! I am here for the funeral!"

My friends almost fell down when I yelled at them. They looked at me as if I had three heads and they were terrified. After this, to our amazement, the ghosts turned their heads, looking back to the funeral.

Tom asked, "Hey man, What do we do? I am scared."

I said to everyone. "Attened the funeral."

Lori asked, "Attend the funeral? From here?"

I responded, "Yes, from here."

My friends really thought I lost it, however they did not run. They all stood there. I stood there. We watched with amazement and then, after a little while, the ghosts disappeared. We were all pale and we were scared, however, we did stay.

After about thirty minutes we left the graveyard, headed off to our favorite pizzeria and we discussed the vision that we saw. In the past, we would all try to forget what happened. Now, it was a different story. However, make no mistake about it, we were all terrified.

Mike asked, "So let me get this straight. You say that she is not evil, but yet, she haunts us with these visions?

I said, "My friends, All I am saying is, I think Tori is trying to tell us her story. I don't think people gave her the time of day. They were all going to get a haunting. My suggestion is, when we go, instead of just looking for a thrill, listen with your hearts, and see if she says anything else."

Dianna replied, "I always believed that there is more to the story. I don't know why."

Melissa said, "Troy, listen, I believe you. I think your kind heart is getting to you more than your head. I suggest that we still use caution."

I said, "Absolutely. I am not saying that we will not get terrified. I am only asking that we listen and see."

Mike said, "That funeral really did me in, man. I am in need of a break."

Everyone nodded and I said, "I understand."

We all took a break for the rest of the year and focused on our school work so we could graduate. We were all dreading winter's approach as we were never a fan of winter. Due to the season's change we started to make our plans for winter hang outs to pass the time. In this time, however, I did ponder the events that took place, and I decided that when spring first came, I would make a private visit to the cemetery.

CHAPTER 7

A FIGHT, WHAT FIGHT?

It was now the year nineteen ninety five and my friends and I passed the winter's time with some fun things to do. We did things like, indoor bumper cars, went to movies, had jam out sessions, went off to each other's houses, and other things you would expect teens to do. We were successful passing the winter's time and it flew by.

When the first day of spring arrived, I was planning to make good on my private visit to the grave. I decided that I would go on Saturday, in the morning, so I could have plenty of time with my friends afterward. I borrowed my mom's car, stopped for breakfast pancakes, and headed off to the cemetery.

I arrived at the graveyard, and then I went inside to visit the headstone of Tori first. I reached out my hand and I touched the headstone, looked down, and saw my guitar pick. I said out loud, "Tori, what happened to you?

I do not think you are evil. I am convinced that there is more to your story."

After this I turned and headed over to the crypt. I reached out my hand and I touched the old wooden door. Then, as I was there, thinking, I heard a voice again. "I am perfectly okay today. It is a very nice day." As always, I was overcome with fear. This time, I defied my fear. I turned around and asked, "Tori?" Of course there was no answer. Then I said, "Tori, I have an idea, wait here, and I will return."

I left the cemetery and drove down the street, to a pizzeria that was about one mile from there. I went into the pizzeria and got a small pepperoni pizza to go. I left the pizzeria and I returned to the cemetery. I went inside the grave and sat on a bench that was there. I said, "Tori. I am back. Let's have lunch."

My friends, I did not believe that Tori was going to eat a piece of pizza with me for one second. It was the gesture that counted. I sat on the bench and I ate the whole pizza. After I was done I said, "That was a great lunch. That pizzeria is very good." Then, I heard a voice, "It's a very nice day today. I would have loved a piece."

I was chilled to the bone. Again, defying my fears, I said, "It is a great day today. I will return soon."

I left the cemetery to go chill with my friends. During this time we did not have anything unusual happen to us. It was quiet. We were busy, as school was drawing near to the end, and graduation would be soon.

A few weeks have passed and my friends and I decided that we would make another trip to the infamous cemetery. This time my friends decided to give me a chance to see if my theory was correct. I was not sure about my theory, however, it just seemed to be a gut feeling. We went to the cemetery about eight o' clock at night. When we arrived we explored the church. We never did that before.

I said, "Hey all, look at this."

Everyone came over and we saw what looked like tool marks, as if the church was broken into before. The doors were locked so it was obvious that these events took place in the past.

Melissa said, "I heard it said that cults broke in here to try and speak with Tori."

Everyone got creeped by that statement. I said, "I remember you telling me that once, Melissa."

Melissa replied, "We are obviously witnessing the markings the intruders made."

Mike said, "I could never break in there to try and talk with a ghost. That creeps me out way too much."

Dianna agreed saying, "That is too crazy. No way!"

After about five minutes we heard the church bell go off. We jumped three feet, our hearts, in our throats, paralyzed, with fear. I said, "No way that bell rings again!"

Mike said, "That's nothing!" See this?"

We turned and we looked, turning white as if we were ghosts. We were frozen with fear. We saw ghosts, and they started to enter the church. Then we heard, as if it was the pastor, giving a sermon."

Melissa was so scared she could not move. The rest of us looked at each other, wide eyed, frozen terror, awed, with amazement. This time, we were so terrified that we ran to the hill for about an hour. I was trying to test my theory, however, that sighting really got to me.

Chris asked me, "Troy, any theory about that?"

I told everyone, "The only thing that comes to my mind is the wake. Perhaps Tori is showing us something with that."

Melissa said, "That makes sense, however, I am not returning to find out."

Everyone said, "No way. After this passes we are leaving."

I agreed with them. I said, "Well, tonight I am too scared to go back. That got to me. I admit it."

After about an hour passed we returned to the cars and we had a surprise. We saw that Dillian, and his crew were there now. I thought, "This is just great. I want to get out of here."

We arrived at the cars and sure enough Dillian started to pick a fight with me.

Dillian said, "Punk! Fancy seeing you here. Are you here to see a ghost? I am going to make you a ghost!"

My friends jumped in saying, "Dillian, we have no time for this. We need to leave right now."

Dillian pushed me. I tried to stay calm and caught my breath. I said, "Dillian, listen, we all need to leave right now. I'm serious."

Dillian replied, "No way, I have been waiting too long to knock your lights out."

I said, "Dillian, you have no idea what is even happening here."

Dillian said, "What? Ghosts? You loser, you think I buy that junk?"

I said, "Dillian, trust me."

Dillian pushed me again, I was starting to get mad, and then defend myself, then, to our horror, all of us heard a female voice. "Don't you touch him!" We all looked around and no one saw anyone.

The voice said, "You leave him alone!"

Dillian's friends started to say, "Dill, let's just get out of here. Come on."

Dillian said, "Not without knocking his lights out first!"

His friends said, "Forget it, man, let's just go."

Dillian pushed me again and then the female voice shouted, "Get out of here! I can get very angry!"

Dillian turned pale. He looked at me and said, "You just got lucky pal. When we meet again, you're dead."

As Dillian was getting into the car with his friends, the female voice shouted, "You will not hurt him! Now, I am mad!"

Dillian and his friends left the cemetery, and as he was leaving, the car lost control, smacked into a tree, the car was on fire. I yelled, "We have to help them! Let's go! Mike, call for help!"

My friends and I ran over to them, pulled them out of the car, Mike left for a pay phone, to call for help.

We all stayed with Dillian and his crew, doing our best to help, trying to somehow control the flames. Nothing worked and there was no water. Then we started to hear sirens. The ambulance, a firetruck, and the police arrived. Dillian was crying and his friends were very scared.

The firefighters did a great job putting the fire out. Dillian and his friends were put into the ambulance, the police did their job sorting everyone out. I told the police that I did not know Dillian and that I only saw him in high school. I told them the car just lost control, and that they were not speeding. I did not want Dillian to get into any trouble. It worked, and no one got in trouble.

My friends and I left the scene and we hung out at the field for the rest of the night. We loved that field because it was very quiet. We were all talking about the event that took place.

We did not know what to make of the night, or the fight, or the crash. My friends were baffled that I saved Dillian, his friends, and that I did not turn them in.

Mike said, "Well, Troy, looks like a ghost defends you, man."

I said, "We do not know that for sure."

Tom jumped in, "Hey, face it, you were defended, dude, it's way too coincidental."

Dianna said, "Yeah, that's wicked cool."

Melissa was silent. I asked her if everything was okay. Melissa said, "I am fine, just shaken up."

I told my friends, "I think that if I was defended, it would have happened for any of us. Not just me."

My friends were silent. I continued, "Seriously, I think it would have been any one of us."

Tom said, "Hey dude, no worries, it's still way cool."

I laughed, "Well, it is a strange coincidence."

After that we all discussed the meaning of the ghosts going inside of the church. I proceeded to tell my friends that I believed that Tori was trying to tell the story about the wake. We all wondered if there was anything at the wake that made her mad. However, there was no way of telling for sure and the records I had did not reveal anything about it.

We all returned home for the night and when the next morning came I had a phone call from Dillian's mom. She told me that Dillian requests to see me at the hospital. I told her I would be there.

I arrived at the hospital and Dillian was in tough shape. We looked at each other and then we spoke.

Dillian said, "Dude, you helped me. Why?

I said, 'I never had a problem with you. I did not want you to get in trouble either."

Dillian broke out in tears. "You saved my car too. The insurance is covering it. It is due your report to the police and they are treating it as a normal accident."

I said, "I am glad to hear that."

Dillian said further, "I will not be able to walk for about one month. I am temporarily paralyzed. The doctors said this can be treated. So I have hope."

I said, "Hey, I am in your corner too."

Dillian said, I am so sorry for everything. I don't want to hurt you anymore."

I said, Dillian, forget it, there is nothing to forgive. Nothing happened, except this."

Dillian said, "I know. I feel so bad now."

I told Dillian, "Forget it. You just concentrate on recovery. We all need to work for graduation time."

Dillian reached out and we shook hands. Not only was there a fight that never happened, we became friends from that time going forward. I was very glad that Dillian was okay and that he had hope of recovery.

As I was leaving I was approached by Dillian's mother. She started to speak with me saying, "I want to thank you and your friends for saving my son's life. If not for you all, I probably would be burying him in a week." She started to cry.

I said, "I am very glad he is safe, ma'am"

She said, "The thought of losing your own child is very overwhelming. I am so happy that he is alive."

I said, "It was an honor to help them all, ma'am."

She continued, "I sure hope that the doctors can help him walk again."

I said, "He is strong, I am sure they will be able to help him. He will walk again."

She hugged me and bid me farewell. She also said that I could go over to their house and visit them anytime. I would always be welcome as a very good friend. I was very happy for them all. I looked forward to the day Dillian was walking again.

Monday morning came and I arrived at school for the day's work. As I entered the other teens turned, looked at me, looked at my friends, and they all started to clap their hands. They cheered us on and they were all yelling, "To the heroes of the school!"

We did not know what to make of this. We were all stunned that this was happening. This time my friends and I got very popular with the teens and the teachers. My friends and I were glad to have helped. Then we were stopped by a lot of people because they wanted autographs from us.

My friends and I signed many autographs. We were not allowing this to get to our heads. We were, however, glad a life was saved, even if the person did not like me at first. I left that all behind me. Moving

forward, I was a friend of Dillian, and everyone knew it.
Everybody was happy and celebrated the new
friendship.

        For the next few weeks my friends and I were
studying very hard to pass all of our classes and
graduate high school. We all hung out when we could,
however, we realized that graduation would be upon us
soon. So we decided to put some of our hangout times
down for a little while to study. After all, we all still had
another summer to go through with each other. We were
all looking forward to that as well.

CHAPTER 8

EVIL? OR NOT EVIL?

The month of May approached and all of us knew that this was the month that we heard was Tori's favorite month. We decided that we would head off to visit the legendary graveyard very soon. Also, my friends were still interested to see if my theory was correct.

Due to homework and a fast approaching graduation we decided to make the trip in two weeks. We were all buckled down to pass our exams and be done with high school. We were all looking forward to that. Also we decided that, with the summer ahead, we would be able to go a few more times as well.

During this time I made a trip to the Exeter Town Hall. I wondered if the clerk had any information about the wake that took place for Tori. I was able to borrow my mom's car and I made the trip, after school, Wednesday.

I got out of the car and I saw the same clerk that gave me the records that she could. She was very happy to see me. I was excited to learn something if I could.

She said, "Welcome back my boy. What brings you here today?"

I replied, "I was wondering if you, by any chance, know what happened at Tori't wake. I am not asking for records."

The clerk replied, "The only thing that I ever heard about was, a fire almost broke out during the wake. The pastor accidentally bumped into a candle stand, it fell, and it landed next to a very flammable liquid. If not for the parrish the church may have exploded."

I was shocked, "So if the people could not do anything, many lives would have been lost?"

The clerk said, "Exactly. That is the only thing I ever heard. I do not know much else."

I said, "Madam, thank you, you were of great help."

She said, "Well, I am glad to have helped." She smiled.

I bid her farewell and I headed over to see if Rick, the property manager, was working. When I arrived he saw me and he greeted me with a handshake. I asked him if he knew about the fire that almost broke out at the wake.

Rick said, "From what I understand it is true. I have to go inside that church at times and I can see leftover burn marks from that. Most of it was repaired. The marks are small now."

I was very intrigued, "That is very interesting."

Rick said, "I have a little time. I will show you."

I gulped. "That would be very cool sir, thank you."

We left, taking separate cars and went to the church. We arrived and Rick pulled out his keys, unlocked the doors, and we entered the church. It was musty smelling, old, spider webs, old wood, and yet the past was haunting in itself.

Rick brought me to the spot and said. "Tori faced this way during the wake. The candle stand was here. This is where it knocked over and the fire almost went out of control."

I was stunned looking at this piece of history. "I find this very amazing sir. This really speaks to me."

He said, "Many lives were saved due the bravery of the parrish putting the fire out. They did not have a fire department in those days."

Learning that was highly amazing. I mean, I knew it, I just did not put two and two together. Now, the scene really spoke to me. Then, to my horror, I realized, many lives were saved here, Dillian and his friends' lives saved there. I almost fainted.

When we left the church I thanked Rick for showing me all of that history. We bid each other farewell and I drove away to see my friends. I was looking forward to seeing them.

When I saw my friends we all were very happy to hang out. We fist bumped and hugged, we were all very chill. I started to tell them what I had learned from the clerk. I did not tell them about the church.

They were amazed at learning this. Mike asked, "So let me get this correct. Scare the living daylights out of us, to tell us about the fire. And you're trying to convince me this is not evil?

I said, "Perhaps it's the only way Tori can tell us her story. We can not guarantee that we will not be scared."

Mike said, "No disrespect, but I am not buying it. I also hate the fact that a fire is linked to a haunted cemetery. That reminds me of a ouija board."

Melissa asked, "You played one of those things?"

Mike replied, "No, but I know a few people that did. The outcome was not great either. And somehow, a fire is always involved somewhere along the lines. Dillian's car caught fire. How about that?"

I have to admit that creeped us out for a minute. We had an awkward silence for about five minutes. Melissa ended up saying, "Well there are many fires that are accidental. It does not make someone a demon. I mean, we never did an ouija board, have we?"

I said, "Never."

The others said, "No way, I swear, too scary."

Mike said, "Well I am sorry, but I am not convinced that this is not evil. Listen to me now. Let us take a break for now. We have graduation soon. We do not need anything now. It has been quiet, thankfully."

I asked Mike, "What about two weeks?"

Mike said, "I may, I may not. You all can, I may stay out. I will not guarantee that I am going."

All of us sighed. I said, "Mike just give this a chance. I don't think she is a demon."

Mike said, Well, I am too creeped out right now. I just need to calm down."

We all respected Mike's wishes and we hoped that he would change his mind. My friends were trying to see if my theory was correct. I was very sad that Mike got scared like this. However, this may have been his final straw. As humans, we all have one. We just let Mike be, and when the night was over, we returned to our studies for school.

A few days have passed and Mike was not himself. We began to worry about him. I told the crew that I will have a talk with him to see if he was okay. His school work was normal, he was studying for graduation, his grades, awesome, however, he was definitely not himself.

I stole that same night and visited Mike at his house. I knocked on his door and he let me in. I proceeded to speak with him to find out what was wrong.

I said, "Mike, everyone is worried about you. What is wrong?"

Mike answered, "Troy, I love you and the entire crew, you know that. I am just extremely weirded out by the wake seen and the ghosts entering the church. I am also extremely creeped out by Dillian's event and the fire after the crash."

I said, "I did not realize that this was playing with your mind. I am sorry."

Mike said, "Not your fault. I have also been having terrible nightmares."

I asked, "Really, like what?"

Mike said, "Dreams about the church. In my dreams it totally burns down. And the ghosts start chasing me through the woods, blaming me for it. When I think I get away from them, I end up in a graveyard, and they chase me from there."

I could barely say anything. Mike asked, "Do you think Tori is haunting me, man?"

I answered, 'Tori, no. Last year, I would say, yes. This time, I do not think it is Tori."

Mike asked, "How can you be so sure?"

I said, "I can't. However, I do believe that you are so terrified that you are having these dreams by nature. They are occurring because it is so fresh in your mind."

Mike said, "You might be right. Now, I want you and everyone else to listen to me. Please! Stay away from there. There is no reason for any of you to become like me. Forget the place even exists. Let's finish school. I do not want any of you to lose your minds."

I told Mike, "We are still planning to go the night that we planned. I think I will be okay."

Mike replied, "Okay? Are you serious? Dillian almost got killed! His whole crew did!"

I said, "Mike, perhaps you should try and get some rest now. You look very tired."

Mike said, "You are right. I am sorry for snapping at you. I am just scared."

I said, "Hey man, forget about it. We are bro's for life, you snapped at me for one second. Forget it. I understand."

Mike said, "Thanks man."

I told him, "Now you get some rest. I will leave now. I have to study history right now. I need to pass that class."

Mike headed to his room for a good night's sleep. I left his house and returned home to work on my history for school. I was very worried about Mike. I did not realize that this was driving him mad. I was hoping he would not lose his mind as Edna told me some people do.

The next day, after school, I had a phone call from Dianna. She asked me if I could go to her house and speak with her. I told her I would be right over. I got worried about this. Due to the event with Mike, what is wrong with Dianna? Needless-to-say, I greatly hoped she was okay.

I arrived at her house and she greeted me with a hug. The first thing she asked me was Mike's situation. I told her that Mike is traumatized at this point and he needed some time by himself.

Dianna said, "I understand. I am having very weird dreams as well."

I gulped, "You too?"

Dianna replied, "Yes. After Mike brought up the fire, that has been tormenting my mind. I have been having dreams of people dying in a car crash. I woke up with a cold sweat."

I told Dianna, "I do not believe that this is Tori. Last year, yes. This year, no."

Dianna replied, "I don't think it's Tori. I just think I am terrified because of Dillian."

I said, "This is very strange how a fire is working you and Mike up. Mike is in tough shape right now."

Dianna said, "I still want to go with you, when you go."

I asked, "Really?"

Dianna said, "Yes I do. I think you are right. I think there is more to the story. For some reason, I believe that if we learn what happened, these strange things will stop. I am not saying anything about whether Tori is evil or not. I am not sure"

I said to Dianna, "I am not blaming Tori for these occurrences. I believe everything is fresh in our heads. That is why we are having these dreams."

Dianna said, "Have you been having dreams?"

I said, "Absolutely. However, for some reason, I am not scared as I would have been."

Dianna asked, "What dreams have you had?"

I answered, "I dream that I am locked in the crypt. Just like that kid in the early nineteen hundreds. Hey, maybe Tori is mad about that as well! I wonder if there is any history to that!"

Dianna jumped saying, "Yeah! I never thought of that! You may be right!"

I told Dianna, "I need to go back home and study math. We have exams as you well know."

Dianna replied, "I have homework too. I do have to study."

I left Dianna's house, giving her a hug, and telling her that I would see her soon. I returned home and pondered the thought of that crypt and what may have really happened. After about an hour of thinking I began to study for my class exams.

The next day we all met in the morning before our classes and we discussed the latest thought I had meeting with Dianna. All of my friends gulped and they all agreed that something may have happened at the crypt.

Tom said, "Troy! Yeah! You may be on to something! Hey, what if that kid ended up getting killed?"

All of us gulped. I said, "Perhaps Tori saw that and she is extremely mad about that. She passed away young. She would be livid."

Melissa said, "Hey, this is wicked cool. Perhaps we are on to something no one ever really knew about!"

Mike said, "Now we have two ghosts there? That's all we need."

I said, "Mike, we do not know if there are two ghosts there. Tori may just be trying to tell us what happened."

Mike said, "Troy, you're crazy, man. No disrespect, I am telling you, stay away."

I said, "Hey everyone, I will be okay. I am just trying to learn what happened."

Mike said, "We already know what happened. It's time to leave it alone."

I told everyone, "Listen, I am going to see what may have happened. I am not forcing any of you to come with me. I will be fine."

Mike said, "Until you have the living daylights scared out of you."

I told Mike, "Mike, you are in tough shape right now. Just let the time pass, you will be okay."

Melissa said, "Troy is right, just give it time. We are all friends. There is no reason for us to start an argument."

Everyone took a deep breath and we calmed down. We agreed that we would not argue. We all gave each other a hug, and went to class because the school bell rang. We all agreed to meet up after school at our pizzeria.

After school hours came along I headed off to our favorite pizzeria. When I arrived I saw Chris and Lori there first. We all greeted each other with a fist bump, then we started to talk. The cashier said, "May I take your order please?" We all ordered a large pepperoni and sat down waiting for the others.

Chis said, "Troy, Lori and I have an idea. Please hear us out."

I said, "Sure, I will."

Chris said, "I think we should just wait until after graduation and then, we visit Vampire's Grave again. This way, everyone can clear their minds. We have been through a lot, man."

Lori said, "Troy, Dillian and his entire crew almost got killed. We know this has everyone terrified. It's too creepy."

I sat and I thought about this. Perhaps this was needed, and it was fair for everyone. As we sat, everyone else came in, ordered their food and sat down with us.

Chris told everyone about his idea. Everyone nodded and seemed to be in agreement. Mike was still a bit skeptical as I imagined he would be. Lori told everyone that she was terrified about the fire as well.

I said, "It is probably wise to wait until we graduate first. After all, we do not need anything bad to happen before that. Perhaps I am just in a rush."

Lori said, "Troy, we respect your theory, however, you could be wrong."

I said, "I know that Lori. I am only going by a gut feeling. However, I want all of you to realize that I know that I could be wrong."

Mike said, "I already think you are wrong Troy. I still respect your theory. I just don't want our cars crashing and catching on fire."

I said, "I know. Listen, everyone, I will see Edna on this matter over the weekend. Perhaps she knows some stuff about this."

Dianna said, "Please, do not tell her about our nightmares."

I said, "No, no, you all, I am going to ask her about the boy that was locked in the crypt. I think I will wait until we graduate. We only have a few weeks left. I sure can use more study time."

Everyone smiled and it appeared that a great relief came upon all of them. I smiled and was very happy that we came into an agreement. I really thought we may have ended up in an argument. My friends were happy that I was to visit Edna and see if I could get more information.

Saturday approached and I headed to Edna's house. As always, she greeted me with a smile, let me in, and made us some coffee. We sat down in the kitchen and we started to talk.

I said, "I am about to graduate in a few weeks."

Edna said, "I know dear, that must be exciting."

I said, "It is. I am highly looking forward to it."

Edna asked, "Have you been staying away from that cemetery, my friend?"

I said, "At this time, yes, I have another history question for you. You may know the answer."

Edna replied, "Of course."

I asked her, "Do you by any chance know about a boy that was locked in the crypt, about early nineteen hundreds?"

Edna said. "Yes. From what I was told, the caretaker went mad while he was working there. A boy was annoying him and the caretaker lost his mind. He grabbed the boy and locked him in the crypt for three days."

I gulped, "Did the boy actually die afterward?"

Edna replied, I don't believe so. However, the boy passed away a while ago. He is not even buried there. I do not have any information as to how he died."

I told Edna, "Edna, you may think I am crazy, I do not think Tori is evil."

Edna replied, "Of course not, son. She is angry. Angry yes, evil, no. There is a big difference."

I proceeded to tell Edna, "I think that Tori is trying to tell me her story. All of the events that happened have some link to what transpired."

Edna said, "This is the first time I heard of this. I am not saying that you are crazy. I never knew of Tori trying to say anything. I would advise you to be careful."

I said, "By all means."

Edna asked me, "How do you get this theory?"

I replied, "I don't know. I just have a gut feeling. Call me crazy, I got a pizza and went to the grave. I defied my fear and said, Tory, let's have lunch. I knew she would not really have a piece of pizza with me. It was the gesture that counted. I ate the whole pizza."

Edna asked, "Did anything happen after that?"

I told Edna, "Yes, I heard a female voice. She said it was a pretty day and that she would have loved a piece."

Edna said, "In all of my years, this is the first time I ever heard of this. I have never heard of any teen bringing her a pizza. Every case I ever knew was vandalism, thrills and chills, provoking her, poke fun of, and the likes. Every teen was going there to see a vampire ghost. My boy, you may have struck a chord."

I gulped, "Like, you don't think she likes me, right?"

Edna laughed, "Not in that fashion, silly. No, I mean that showing her kindness may have changed her mind about you. I can not say this is final, however, it is possible. I never heard of anything as to what you have told me."

I responded, "I never thought of it that way. Do you think it is possible that Tori may like my friends?"

Edna said, "I have no idea about that. Do you have a friend that will go to the cemetery with you?"

I answered, "Yes, I do."

Edna said, "I have an idea. Take your friend there and both of you do something nice. Whatever it is you want. See if anything happens that is positive."

I said, "That is a great idea. Dianna is the best choice for this."

I bid Edna farewell after two hours of visiting her. I gave her a hug and thanked her for all her help. She told me to come back anytime. I headed off to Dianna's place to tell her what I learned.

Dianna was very happy to see me when I arrived. I asked her if she would go to the cemetery with me. Dianna was thrilled to go and she did think I was crazy for trying the idea Edna gave me. Dianna was willing to give it a shot.

I have to say that I thought I was crazy. I defied my brain and I brought my acoustic guitar. Dianna brought a candle and we arrived at the cemetery.

When we arrived we went to Tori's headstone. Dianna was the first to speak. Dianna said, "Tori, I do believe that you are trying to tell us your story. I agree with Troy. I do not think you are evil."

I said, "Tori, I brought my guitar. Dianna has a great voice. I sing too. We want to play a song for you."

I started playing the song and Dianna started to sing. I followed Dianna's lead. We sang a song about God, from an old church hymn. Who knows, perhaps the very church that is here, had this song as well.

After the song was over we proceeded to walk over to the crypt. To our surprise we heard a female voice. "It's a very pretty day today. I loved that song."

Dianna was paralyzed with fear. I was shaken up too. I said to Dianna, "Defy your fear, do not run."

Dianna said, "I am not running. I am scared, awed, surprised, wow!

I said, "I am awed too."

We both stopped dead in our tracks. I went over to the bench and we played two more songs. After the songs were over we heard a female voice again saying, "It's a great day today. I am perfectly okay. I love your songs."

Dianna wanted to run. I could tell. I told Dianna again, "Defy your fear, don't run."

Dianna said, "This is just amazing. I think I am going mad."

I said, "I don't think so. But thanks for coming with me. Let's get some dinner and meet everyone else.

Dianna said, "Yeah, sounds wicked cool."

As I was leaving the cemetery, I looked around and I said, "Tori, no. It's an excellent day today. I will be back again."

Dianna and I left the cemetery to get some dinner. We did not have much money so we went to Mcdevon's and got a chicken sandwich with french fries. We ate there discussing the event. I was awestruck by what transpired and so was Dianna.

I said to Dianna, "Now, I do not believe Tory is evil at all."

Dianna said, "I don't either."

I replied, "Angry yes, evil, no. There is a difference."

Dianna asked me, "Troy, what do you hope to accomplish with all of this?"

I answered, "I just want to know what happened. I think that something very bad happened that made her very angry. I could be wrong. I just believe there is more to the story. I also think that if I listen, she will tell me."

Dianna said, "Troy I agree with you all the way. For some reason I believed with all of my heart that there is more. However, we should use caution."

I told Dianna, "Of course I am."

Dianna also said, "We should not tell anyone about this yet. I don't think it is time."

I said, "I agree. I will tell them what I learned from Edna and the boy that was locked in the crypt."

Dianna said, "That's cool. They will want to know about that. I am sure of it."

Dianna and I ended up meeting our other friends at Mike's house. They were eager to learn what I found out when I was with Edna. I had to keep silent about Dianna, and my private visit to the cemetery. I felt bad about that, however, I did not believe it was time for that yet.

Tom asked, "So Troy, what did you learn with Edna?"

I said, "It is true about the boy getting locked in the crypt. He was locked for three days. The caretaker went mad working there, I was told. The boy was annoying him and the crime occured."

Mike asked, "So did the boy die? Are we dealing with another ghost?"

I said, "Edna said she did not believe the boy died. However, the boy did die a while ago and he is not even buried there."

Mike replied, "So we could be dealing with another ghost."

I told Mike, "I do not believe that is the case. Perhaps something else happened to the crypt."

Melissa said, "Troy, we are probably never going to find out. I agree with Mike, let's leave this alone."

I responded, "You may be right. Perhaps I should put this topic down."

Mike said, "Good. Leave it alone, man. You may be going mad. I do not want to see that. None of us do."

I said, "I think I am okay. I am going to stay away for now so we can graduate. Until then, let's have some fun tonight."

Everyone said, "Yeah, now you're talking!"

We decided to go back to Massachusetts and go to the amusement park. We had a great time riding on the coasters and just forgetting about the hauntings. Yes, it was a great time. I would say, this was probably the best time we had in about one month due to the events.

Of course, after the amusement park was over, we did not want to stop hanging out. So we decided to go back to the quiet field for some drinks and to chill for the rest of the night. We all got home very late. After that we decided that we would use the rest of our time to study so we can all graduate.

CHAPTER 9

ANOTHER SUMMER?

Graduation day finally came and we were very excited about the event. My friends and I worked very hard to pass all of our classes and our exams. Our grades were fantastic and I was very proud of everyone. Now the day has arrived that we will walk the stage to receive our diplomas.

We were all seated in the auditorium and as you all know we sat through several speeches, principal, valedictorian, certain teachers, you all know, the ceremony. Then the time came to get our names called to get our diplomas. As I was sitting there, I turned to look at my parents, and to my surprise, I saw Edna, and Kenny. I was shocked to see that they came to my graduation. I teared up very much.

My name was finally called and the crowd went wild when I walked across the stage. It was the same with my friends as well. We were cheered by all of the others the most. I knew it was because we saved Dillian and his friends' lives when the car crashed and caught fire. The others did treat us as, "Heroes Of The School."

After the ceremony, my friends and I had to return to our own houses to celebrate with our own families before we could get together. When I got home I saw my family, food, cake, and Edna with Kenny.

I said, "Edna! Edna! You came!"

Edna said, "I would not have missed it for the world."

I said, "Kenny! Kenny! I can't believe you came!"

Kenny said, "I had to come and see Tori's friend walk the stage."

I asked, "Did Edna tell you what happened?"

Kenny said, "She sure did!"

I asked both of them, "How did you tell my dad we met?"

Edna replied, "From our favorite pizzeria, my friend."

I said, "Thanks for keeping the secret. I would be grounded for weeks."

Both of them laughed and Kenny said, "I would not have missed your ceremony for the world. You are now considered a friend of the family.

I almost fainted learning this. I mean, after all, to me, Kenny was practically a celebrity in my eyes. Being a distant relative from one of the most famous legends Rhode Island ever has is a remarkable thing. It is safe to say that I looked up to Kenny a great deal.

The party at my house was held for about three hours. Of course everyone had to take pictures of me, and with me. I hated pictures being taken of me, however, I knew it was necessary. I had a great time chilling with friends and family during my party.

After the party was over I helped my parents clean up. They thanked me for lending them a hand and not just darting off to see my friends. My dad liked Edna and Kenny saying they were very nice. He wondered why I never spoke about them. I told my dad, "I just did not think the friendship went this far. This was highly unexpected." My dad was chill about that. I mean, after all, no one lied, Edna and I did meet at our favorite pizzeria.

Evening arrived and I went to meet up with my friends. We decided to meet at the field just to talk about our day and our future. I have to say we were confused at this time as to what would become of us. We were all so busy jamming and hanging out, we did not put much thought to this.

Melissa asked, "So what is to become of our crew now?"

I said, "We move forward together, we are friends forever."

Dianna said, "My only nightmare now is losing all of you."

Mike said, "Not happening, Dianna."

Dianna started to cry, I said, "I know we have to get jobs, however, we will still hang out, right?

Everyone agreed, Melissa said, "Sure, we can't be on the clock forever."

It is safe to say that we were in shock about this night. This never crossed our minds before. What will become of our beloved crew now? This was different. There is no more high school. It is now, jobs, secondary school, or trade school, we had a lot to think about. We pulled out our drinks, and our conversations were a "what if," scenario for the entire night.

We had a good time during our hang out, however, it was slightly depressing. We knew that life would take over at some point. We just hoped that it would take a while before life claimed us in the busy world.

I said, "Well, I know that we still have this summer, So let us hang out and chill when we can."

Melissa said, "I am returning to work at the bakery. I have a day shift now."

Mike said, "I am going to be a mechanic. That is a day job already."

Lori said, "I am going to try and work at a grocery store for the time being. I do not know what I want to do yet."

Chris told everyone, "I got a job at a moving company right now. It is a day job.

Tom said, "I am going to work at a store for now."

Dianna said, "I have an interview at a cafe. We will see what happens."

I said, "My dad is training me to work on cars. I will be working at his shop. I want to work as a mechanic too."

Melissa said, "Ok, enough of this! Let's party!"

We all yelled, "YEAH!" Throwing our drinks saying, "Cheers."

We had a great time for the rest of the night. The depression left and it was as school was not over yet. We chilled at the field until the very late hours. We talked about many things other than jobs and the future. It was time to celebrate.

A week had now passed and we started to see that our jobs were not that bad. We still had plenty of hours to hang out. The difference now would be, sometimes one of us could not make it due to work. However, that did not happen too much. We were relieved because, at first, we thought it was over.

The time came and I was pondering Tori Brown and Vampire's Grave. I was still curious if there was more to the story. For example, was she in a coma, and did her dad kill her by accident? I knew that the cold weather would preserve a body. Since the medical profession was not as advanced back then, that would make sense. The townsfolk, having no idea about that science, could make a confusing accusation of vampirism and kill her accidently.

All I knew was the cemetery was haunted with a traumatizing incident. There is a high chance that there is a vampire ghost there that was very angry. With all of this, I wanted to know why. Of course during these thoughts, I knew that I could be wrong and it was a dead end.

I went to my bedroom and I pulled out all my records again. I read through them all to see if there was anything I missed. Did the records speak of anything that no one saw? To my dismay, I did not find anything new.

Saturday was a day I had off. Tom came over to my house and we chilled a bit. The next thing I know he asked me the question.

Tom asked, "Troy, are we still going to the grave and see more hauntings and chills?"

I said, "I am still going, however, I still do not believe Tori is evil. Remember?"

Tom said, "I remember. I still think you may be wrong. I think she is, man, sorry."

I said, "You have a right to your opinion. I am not mad at all. I could be wrong."

Tom said, "Well according to Mike, you are. He is still struggling. Not as bad as before."

I replied, "So Mike got to your mind."

Tom said, Hey, I am just looking at the case. If Tori is not evil, Mike would be fine by now."

I did not know what to say at this point. To tell you the truth, a high flash of doubt crossed my mind. I proceeded with caution however, because I did not want to start making accusations for no reason. I still had cases where I saw that Tori was not evil. I kept a clear mind.

The crew ended up coming to my house with the exception of Mike. For some reason they seemed to return to their old ways about Vampire's Grave. I was devastated about this. We were all going and they wanted a haunting.

As we were in the car, my heart was not in it. I do not believe Dianna's heart was in it either. She was quiet. All I could think of was "I hope they are not going to do anything foolish.

I said to Tom, "Tom, please do not wreck the place."

Tom said, "Dude, of course I am not. I just want a thrill, man, that's all."

I was there as more of a peer pressure case. I had a feeling that a great provocation was about to occur, My friends were not acting right. It was as if they lost their mind. They were all laughing and it was different. It was as if they had a mischievous laugh. I wanted to leave, however, as fate would have it, I stayed.

When we got to the cemetery I told Tom, "Tom, chill out a bit, you are scaring me."

Tom replied, "Relax man, I told you I am not going to do anything."

Melissa was acting strange too. I thought this was a little different for her. She was always more mellow. All of my friends were hyper. I said with a very soft tone, "Tori, I am not in this."

Everyone went into the cemetery and Tom started to shout. I want to see a vampire! Where is the ghost?

Melissa and everyone else was laughing.I was questioning if they were making fun of me. This was not like my friends. However, they were serious.

Tom continued, "Hey vampire! Come out and play!"

I yelled, "Tom! You sound insane. Stop this nonsense!"

Tom replied, "Dude, I am just having a little fun. Calm down."

My friends were all looking around with keen interest. They went nuts. Their laugh was now, as if they were insane. I started to wonder if this is what Edna was talking about.

Tom yelled, "Vampire, I am starting to get bored!"

Everyone finally settled down and got quiet. Then Tom said, "Nothing is happening. Nothing at all. Perhaps Mike can go back to normal."

Now I understood what got my friends so worked up. It was Mike. Not directly, but indirectly due to Mike's case. Everyone felt horrible for Mike. I did too, however, I did not believe it was Tori. It is safe to say that my friends were mad and this explained their behavior.

Suddenly, there was an ear piercing shriek! We were all silent, looking around, and then again, after that, there was a female voice, "You want to see a ghost!? You want to see a vampire!?"

I was very scared, not knowing what to do. I just wanted out. We were all gripped with terror. Then, to our horror, appeared a ghost, about nineteen years of age, in a Victorian dress showing herself at the crypt.

The female yelled, "You want to see a vampire!?" She said this with a very horrifying yell.

She started to walk toward us. Then she opened her mouth to reveal the fangs of a vampire. She walked toward Tom.

Tom was shaking to his bone, my friends were all gripped with fear. Tom said, "Okay, let's bolt!" I am out of here!"

The ghost arrived and she looked at me, ignored me, and continued towards Tom. She shrieked again with a very horrible pitch. She was angry and I did not blame her. She taunted Tom, "No, come here, you want to see a vampire! Come to me my darling!" Her voice echoed as if we were in the mountains.

Everyone was running out of the cemetery and I followed them. I wanted to leave. And once again, the cars did not start so we proceeded to the rock as before. The ghost followed us a little ways taunting us, "Don't run! You want to see a ghost! I want you to join me here, forever! Come back! Come back!"

When we got to the rock we were all catching our breath. I said, "Well, Thanks a lot Tom.I hope you are satisfied."

Tom said, "Hey, I got my thrill."

I asked Tom, "What has gotten into you, man?"

Tom said, "See, she is evil, dude! This just proves it!"

I said, "This proves nothing! You all went into the graveyard in a frenzy, provoking the living daylights out of her!"

Tom said, "I did, and this proves she is a ghost witch! Come to your senses! It is time to take a break!"

I said, "All of you are mad because of Mike! I see it now! I am not saying that Mike is to blame! However, I see that you are all angry! What did you hope to accomplish?"

Tom said, "To prove to you that you are losing your mind! You do not need to continue with your theory!"

I was devastated. I thought my friends respected my opinion on the matter. Perhaps I was wrong. I sort of felt betrayed and that this event was a trap. I kept a level head about it though, because I knew my friends were upset about Mike.

I told them, "Well, I hope you are all happy now. Let's just hope you do not have any experiences for three months now."

Tom said, "Dude, I am over it. I convinced myself that it's all in our heads."

At this point I think that I understood what Edna meant about losing your mind at this cemetery. This was all very odd for my friends. They never acted this way before, except the first time we came, because we did not know if this was truly haunted.

When the hour was up we all went back to our cars and they started up. We slowly backed out and drove down the road. As we were leaving, I said very softly, "I am sorry, Tori."

We went to the field and my friends were still wild. They were not bringing up the event but talking about other things. I felt like I was an odd ball during this hang out. This was the first time that I felt alone.

The next day came and I went to the cemetery, borrowing my mom's car once again. I had to go because I was feeling very bad about last night. I really hoped Tori would not be mad at me. I had to find out if she was.

On the way to the graveyard I stopped at the pizzeria in Exeter. I bought a small pepperoni pizza and continued to the site. When I arrived, I ran to the headstone of Tori. When I got there I started to cry. I said, "Tori, I am sorry for my friend's behavior last night. I was not in on that, nor did I think they were going to do that. I brought lunch again. I hope I can eat it here."

I went to the bench and I ate the whole pizza. After I ate, I got up and said, "I love that pizzeria." Then I started to get chills. I heard a female voice, "It's a very pretty day today. I know that, silly."

I was awed as I usually was. I turned around and I asked, "Tori?"

Of course there was no answer. Everything was silent. I was trying to cheer myself up. Then I heard a female voice again saying, "I would have loved to have a piece of the pizza with you."

I have to say that once again I had to defy my fear. I was chilled to the very bone. I said, "I have to go to work tomorrow. I will be back soon."

As I was leaving I heard the female voice, "It's a very pretty day today. I am perfectly okay."

I said, "No Tori, today is an excellent day."

I left the cemetery and returned home. I wanted to chill out by myself for the rest of the day. When I got home, I went into the basement and jammed on my guitar for a few hours. After that, I went into my room and I watched a movie.

Monday approached and I went to work in my dad's auto mechanic shop. He had me doing the normal start off, entry level things like, oil change, tire's, batteries, light bulbs. My dad said it would be better if I faced life with a skill under my belt. He told me to go to college, however, having a skill would be a great back up if all else failed.

The hours at my dad's shop were Monday through Friday, eight until five o' clock. I had the weekends off so that was great for hanging out with my friends. It was different not to have school any longer. I was adjusting to life anew as a high school graduate.

Wednesday night came and I had a phone call from Dianna. She was chilled to the bone with the tone of her voice. She asked to come by my house and I told her she could.

Dianna arrived and gave me a hug. She was shaking and I got very nervous. I proceeded to speak with her.

I asked, "Dianna, what happened?"

Dianna said, "Troy, everyone, except Mike, lost their jobs today, including me."

I replied, "No way."

Dianna continued, "The strange thing was, it happened at the same hour for every one of us. My boss went berserk on me, and fired me."

This time, I knew this had to be a vexation from Tori. This was way too much of a coincidence. Everyone at the same hour? That is impossible.

I said, "I don't know what to say. This is extreme."

Dianna said, "I know that Tori is behind this."

I said, "I have a feeling you are right. Let us hope you all get jobs again. Very quickly too, for that matter."

Dianna started to cry and I asked her, "Dianna, what got into you the other night?"

Dianna replied, "I don't know. All I know is, Tom was egging us on. For some reason he was in a frenzy and he got us all hyped up. I did not realize that he would go that far."

I said, "Tom. What got into him? I know he is bummed about Mike, however, he was acting insane."

Dianna said, "I lost control too. I am very sorry, Troy."

I told Dianna, "It's okay. Listen, just try and get another job soon. I am sure this will pass."

Then there was a knock on my door. It was Melissa and she asked to chill out for a while. I told her she could. Melissa was shaken up and she was in tears.

I said, "Melissa, You of all people. I thought you would be much better the other night. You introduced me to that graveyard and told me to respect it. I thought you would be the last person to act the way you did."

Melissa said, "I feel very bad, Troy. I know that I acted strange. Tom had me all worked up. I do not know what got into me. I am sorry."

At this point I was thinking about Tom. I questioned what got into him and why he would even want to do this? I was not mad at Tom. I was in question. I knew that Tom could get people worked up if you caught him in the right mood.

I told Melissa, "It's okay Melissa, I guess Tom was in one of those moods."

Melissa said, "I guess he was."

I told Melissa, "Just try and get another job very soon. " I am sure it will pass."

We chilled in my basement for the night. No one else came over to my house. We chilled and we were thinking of a good job hunting strategy to go on so they could return to normal.

When Friday arrived, I was at work, on my lunch break, and a mysterious woman came to the shop. She caught my eye for some strange reason. She asked to speak with me and then, she walked over to me. She told me her name is Jessica.

Jessica said, "You did a great job on my car. Thank you. Here is a twenty dollar tip."

I was shocked, "Thank you ma'am."

Jessica said, "I may have something that will interest you. Follow me to my car."

I went to her car and she pulled out a piece of paper. She said, "I know that Vampire's Grave interests you. This is a clip from the papers, Providence Journal, nineteen fifties. The article talks about a body dump of a young man at Tori's crypt."

I was stunned. I asked her, "Did Edna send you?"

Jessica replied, "No, Kenny sent me."

I gulped, "Thank you ma'am. This article speaks to me. I have a feeling about something. This may be it."

Jessica said, "Listen, I do not believe that Tori is evil either. I have been to that cemetery many times. I have had experiences as well. However, I came to the conclusion that she is not evil."

I said, "That makes me feel better. I guess I am not going crazy."

Jessica said, "You are not. Have a good day. Keep up the great work."

I bid Jessica farewell and when I returned home, I went into my room, and read the article. The article revealed that a young man was killed on Halloween night, and the perpetrators that committed the crime. The article went on to say how the perpetrator's car developed a gas leak, and caught fire, about one quarter of a ways from the graveyard.

I was shocked at this information. The incident with Dillian was the same as well, except for a gas leak. When my friends and I saved Dillian and his friends, there was not one odor of gas. Needless-to-say there were three fires that I have knowledge of. I wondered if this added to Tori's anger, to haunt the cemetery, in the fashion that she did.

I took the article to Mike's house to show him what I learned. I was hoping that he would not be offended, however, I had a feeling that this was somehow linked to his state of mind at this time.

Mike agreed to speak with me. He was doing much better and I was very happy to see that. He opened up his story when he saw the article.

Mike said, "Troy, the criminals in the car, that night, were my dad's very good friends. They went haywire on the guy and wanted to take his life. My dad did not want to have any part of it, so he stayed behind. My dad told me, had he gone along with it, he would have been killed, and I would not be alive. My dad also told me to never visit that cemetery."

I was absolutely shocked. "Mike! I am sorry. I had no idea."

Mike said, "Not your fault. Plus, my dad made the right choice. He is not a murderer. I guess that is why Dillian's incident made me so scared."

I asked Mike, "You said that you had some friends playing a ouija board once. Then, you said something about fire. What happened?"

Mike replied, "Every time they had that board working they seemed to get in touch with something that died by a fire. Then they had bad things happen to them for a few days. They are okay now. That is why the fires are taunting me."

I told Mike, "Wow! Now I understand. I can't believe all of this information. I am so sorry, Mike.

Mike replied, "Again, not your fault. Listen, I am going to stay away from that yard for a while. I am not ready. I just want to work like a normal person right now."

I said, "Mike, I understand. Thank you for sharing that."

Mike asked me, "Please don't tell everyone. Please?"

I told Mike, "Between you and me, man"

Mike said, "Thank you, bro."

I bid Mike farewell and returned to my house with all of this information. Now, I understood why he believed the way he did about Tori. I was not going to interfere with his belief. No way, that is not friendship. I left Mike alone. I did, however, go to my room and ponder the events of everything that happened to us from beginning to where we are at this point in time.

As time passed I wondered if the information I learned was part of anything I needed to know about Tori's case. Thoughts came to me such as, "well, she has haunted this cemetery for years, perhaps this added to her anger, maybe the victim was a relative?" I did not think that I would learn anything new, from the news article that I have. I decided to give up on that, move forward, back to the past, when the tragedy took place.

Friday night came along and all of my friends came to my house. We went to the amusement park in Massachusetts and forgot all about the events that happened to us. We decided it was time to have fun. I did not hold any grudge toward Tom. I knew it was the way he is. He could get people worked up in the right mood. I am glad to say that Tom returned to normal. He was, however, very startled about the mass firing of all his friends. He knew it was Tori's vexation to get revenge. He never spoke about it during this time. I believe he did not want to admit that he acted like a mad man and provoked Tori. I just let Tom be and had fun with my friends.

When Monday arrived, I was at work, wondering how my friends would make out getting new jobs. I could not wait to return home to find out. It is with great joy, that I can tell you, they were successful. They got new jobs doing the same thing as before. The only difference was new working hours. It was not too bad and we still had time to hang out.

I told everyone, "I suggest we leave Tori alone so we can work like normal people."

Everyone nodded and Tom said, "Troy, listen, I am sorry for the trouble I caused. I really do not know what came over me."

I said, "Tom, it's okay. I understand that we get all worked up sometimes."

Tom revealed, "You were right, man. I was very angry about Mike's situation."

I said, "I know."

Tom said, "Well, I respect your view now and I will leave you alone. You do what you wish, learning about Tori."

I was happy and said, "Thank you, Tom. And I am very happy you got a new job as well."

Tom asked, "Do you think Tori will leave us alone?"

I answered, "I believe so. I was told that she does not hold grudges towards people."

Tom was relieved to hear that. I genuinely believed that Tom was truly sorry and he felt bad for the incident. From what I understand, my friends were able to hold their new jobs without incident. We decided to put the graveyard down for a little while, return to work, and have a summer. For all we knew this may be our last summer together.

About three weeks have passed and I made a private visit to the haunted cemetery. I got a little brave this time and went during the night. I did not plan to enter the site, but just to stay at the entrance area, to look around. As I was looking, I saw another person in the cemetery. I was startled, however, I did go in to see who the person could be.

I entered the cemetery being extremely cautious as to not knowing if this person was Tori. I learned that this was a visitor and she was about thirty years of age. She introduced herself to me saying that her name is Alice. Alice was a very nice person to talk to.

I asked her, "Do you think this grave is haunted?"

Alice said, "There is no doubt in my heart that this is haunted. I have had way too many experiences here when I was younger."

I asked Alice, "Are you scared of being in here at night?"

Alice smiled, "Not at all. Tori does not bother me any longer. I have fond memories with my friends, when we were teens, going on ghost hunts."

I asked, "How does Tori leave you alone?"

Alice said, "She is a ghost. She knows way more things now than live humans will ever know in their lifetime. Tori knows who is here to visit, and those who are here for trouble."

I was amazed. "I think there is more to her story than what we know. I don't know why. I believe that something happened here that was very bad, and that is why she is angry."

Alice said, "Maybe this will help. Follow me."

Alice brought me to a headstone that has a square hole, like a window that one can look through. I was amazed to see this and I wondered why I never saw this before.

Alice said, "This may be just a rumor. Nobody can prove this theory, however I heard it said that this window is the gate to her child that died at birth."

I was shocked and said, "Wow!"

Alice had me look through the window and asked, "Do you see that rock?"

I said, "Yes."

Alice said, "I heard that her stillborn lay at rest there. Remember though, this is hearsay. Nobody truly knows. This could be the reason she is upset."

I marvelled at this, however, I had to respect it due to the fact that this may be a rumor. I said, "Perhaps this may be my answer."

Alice said, "Take it with a grain of salt. It adds to the lore but it may be a false tale."

I said, "I will keep this information to myself."

All of a sudden there was a noise and we looked over to the crypt. We saw the figure of a nineteen year old girl, in a Victorian dress, looking at us. I was startled. Alice laughed a gentle laugh.

I asked, "What do you do when you see Tori now?"

Alice answered, "Nothing. I just stay, watch, and I wave. Tori will not bother us."

I was amazed and said, "I never stayed. My friends and I always ran."

Alice answered, "I did too with all of my friends. Times have changed for me now."

I asked Alice, "Do you think there is more to Tori's incident like I do?"

Alice responded saying, "I felt that way for a while. The problem is, I will never know. All we have are the documents of what took place. I do not want to know any more either."

I asked, "Why?"

Alice answered, "That is part of the mystery about this cemetery and what makes it so unique. You know how legendary this graveyard is?"

I said, "No."

Alice continued, "Let me give you an idea. People have driven from all over New England just to come here, and visit this cemetery."

I was amazed, "Wow."

Alice continued, "The most unique thing is, Tori is not your traditional vampire. She is a ghost, a ghost that parades herself as a vampire, as a way to get revenge, because of the accusations against her."

I was in a trance with this knowledge, "I do not actually believe in vampires."

Alice responded, "Neither do I. That is what makes this story so unique. So unique that Hollywood derives some of the horror movies we have due to this cemetery."

That information was a privilege. I never dreamed that I would see a cemetery that was so haunted, that Hollywood would get inspiration to make some movies. I was shocked by that news. I stayed at the cemetery for about one hour speaking with Alice about other things and we bid farewell and parted ways. I returned to my house and Tom, Dianna, Chris, and Lori were there. We chilled out at my house for the rest of the night.

As we were hanging out, I told them everything I learned from Alice. Expect the part of Tori rumored to have a baby. Alice told me to keep that private because nobody knew for sure. My friends were amazed to learn the information.

The next week Melissa came by my house and we went to Tommy's for a burger. We had not been there in a while so it was awesome to eat there. From there Melissa and I went for a run to Vampire's Grave. As we were sitting in the car we were having a discussion.

Melissa said, "From now on when I come here, I want it to be in the same manner I always have in the past. Just look, watch, and see. It was far more peaceful and more thrilling then."

I said, "I get it. Like, how we first visited here when you introduced this place to me."

Melissa said, "Yes. Not coming here to get haunted, thrills and chills, and creeped out, but that old eerie feeling like something is watching you."

I said, "Sounds more exciting that way."

Melissa responded, "Yes, and also more respectful. Last month, I was never so scared in my life. That was too much,"

I said, "Yes, it was, even for me."

Melissa asked, "Are you still going to continue the search for Tori's incident?"

I answered, "I am, however, I will do that on my own time I think."

Melissa said, "Well, I still think you are crazy but hey, we all can get our theories."

I said, "I guess we do."

Melissa continued, "I am sorry for the way I acted that night."

I responded, "It's okay. I was just shocked about the way everyone acted that night."

Melissa said, "Yeah, however, I did not mean to disrespect this place or anybody at all."

Melissa and I talked for about thirty minutes about other things and then we left to meet the others. We all decided for bumper cars and had a regular night. We had a great time and then we all chilled to prepare for the work week.

I was alone in my travels trying to find out the mystery of what happened at Vampire's Grave. One night I was looking at the records and it was later at night. I fell asleep and I had a strange dream.

I saw a small light and a figure of a nineteen year old girl, in a Victorian dress standing there. I was very startled to see this and I wanted to run at first. I defied my fear, I stood there and looked at her. She had long, straight blonde hair, and very light green eyes.

I asked, "Tori?"

She said, "Yes?"

I gulped, I knew it was her. I said, "I am not used to speaking with, or practicing talking with one that has passed before me."

Tori said, "You are not practicing anything." Then she came over and whispered in my ear saying, "You're dreaming."

I was shocked and I asked, "May I ask you a question?"

Tori smiled and said, "Yes."

I asked, "What happened to you, that was so terrible, that made you so angry, to haunt the cemetery all this time?"

Tori answered, "Fear."

I asked, "Fear? You are afraid?"

Tori replied, "I was afraid that I would be forgotten on my passing, when I got very ill. That is why I am very sad."

I asked, "Tori, your status is legendary. How has anyone forgotten about you?"

Tori said, "I was forgotten."

My thoughts were running one mile a minute. I calmed down and asked, 'Why did you seem to leave me alone more during my trips there?'

Tori answered, "You were different."

I marvelled, "Different?"

Tori continued, "Yes, you were different. You did not treat me the same way."

I asked, "How? I went there to see a vampire."

Tori continued, "Perhaps at first. However, you wanted to know about me. I saw you. You wanted to know about me, as a person. Not as a vampire, not as a witch, not a murderer, but as a person. You wanted to know what I was like, when I was alive. Besides, I thought you were kind of cute"

I blushed and said, "Tori, I never saw it that way. I think I understand."

Tori said, "I was forgotten all of these years due to the accusations against me. I was always a vampire in the eyes of many. Now, I am a remembered person."

I was amazed. "Tori, I understand now. To be forgotten was the greatest tragedy. It was even more terrible than the incident itself."

Tori said, "Exactly. Now I am remembered."

I was awestruck and I said. "Tori, perhaps now that you are remembered you can rest."

Tori came over and she took my hands. I said, "You are very cold."

Tori said, "It will pass. I never held hands with a guy before."

I was shocked, and asked, "So, are you nineteen forever?"

Tori said, "Forever and ever. I will never age or be sick again.

I said to her, "You are very pretty."

Tory smiled and whispered, "Thank you."

Suddenly there was a sound and Tori looked away. I looked too because the sound startled me. Tori said, "I have to go now."

I asked her, "Where are you going?"

She replied with a smile, "Silly, I am going to do exactly what you said. I'm going to rest."

She kissed me on the cheek, slowly walked away, and I asked, "Will I ever see you again?"

Tori turned around and asked, "What does your heart tell you?"

After this, the light surrounded Tori, and she disappeared from my sight. I woke up in a cold sweat. I was shocked and amazed by the dream. I wondered if it was even real. The strange thing is, when I got up from my bed, I looked in the mirror and a little lipstick was on my cheek. I fell down on the floor after observing that.

When the day arrived I saw all of my friends. I told them about the dream I had. They were all looking at each other, amazed and bewildered. It is safe to say that they understood the tragedy and they concluded

that this was the answer I was looking for. My friends
agreed that I was visited by Tori herself.

CHAPTER 10

CAN GHOSTS REALLY SING?

The summer was moving right along and the time came when we had to start thinking about any more school, such as college or trade schools. I am not ashamed to admit that we were confused due to not knowing what we wanted to do in life. Not as of yet to say the least.

Mike was already bent on being an established mechanic. I was also in line with Mike because I found working on cars pretty neat. My dad wanted me to go to college and try at least one more thing, before making a decision. My other friends were still trying to figure things out. I have to say that it is a tough choice. Also, it can be very scary as well.

We were still doing our usual things such as, band, hanging out, working, among other things. Since we were working we had money, so we ate out more. That was not a healthy choice, however it happened. We strived to make this a great summer, still wondering if this was our last summer together as a crew.

One night Tom decided to visit me. It was Friday night and he was hyper. I was wondering why. Then I got the question.

Tom asked, "Troy, when are we all going to the cemetery again?"

I asked, "Tom, you are not going to be a nut, right?"

Tom responded, "No way, dude. Not after last time. Besides, your theory was correct. I just want to see if things will be different. I am not going for thrills and chills."

I said, "Okay."

I believed Tom was sincere. After the last time we went everyone got terrified. Added to that, everyone had jobs, so of course we did not want anything bad to happen.

I said to Tom, "I will invite Mike this time. Let's see if he will come."

Tom said, "Great idea."

I went over to Mike's house and he greeted me with a fist bump and a hug. I was very excited to learn that he was doing a lot better. I was nervous about asking him to go with us to the cemetery. I thought it would be cool if everyone went at least one more time.

I asked Mike, "Mike, Tom wants to visit Vampire's Grave again. Do you want to come along?"

Mike responded, "I'm not sure. I have been doing so much better now. I do not want to ruin it."

I said, "No one is going there for thrills and chills this time. This is to look around and have a visit. It's different."

Mike told me, "Let me think about it."

I told Mike, "Okay. I will give you time. Respect if you choose not to go."

After that I went out with Dianna to see a movie and get burgers from Tommy's. We were having a good time. We engaged in conversation about the events.

Dianna said, "It must be wicked cool to have a visitation from Tori. I am so amazed by your dream."

I said, "It was remarkable Dianna. I can't explain it."

Dianna replied, Do you really think Tori will leave us alone during our visit there? " I want to see her, however, in a different way."

I said, "I would like to see her too. Not in the old fashion way though, but in this new understanding."

Dianna replied, "Yeah, that's wicked cool. I love this new understanding."

I said, "Dianna, I never believed in vampires. I barely even thought of ghosts before. I just did not think Tori was evil. There was something about her haunting that place. I just did not know how to explain it."

Dianna replied, "I understand. Trust me, I totally see it."

We left Tommy's to return to my house and we met up with the entire crew. We jammed some songs and we drank for the night. Everyone crashed at my place. It felt great having the normal crew back. We were all in our right minds and having a new understanding about the matters of the cemetery.

Mike said, "I will go with you all. I want it to be different this time. I am talking about no one acting up."

Tom said, "Mike, don't worry about it."

Everyone nodded in agreement. This agreement had Mike at peace with going to the infamous cemetery. Melissa said, "Mike, there is no way I am acting up again."

Dianna asked, "I wonder if we will see anything?" How about you, Troy?"

I said, "Perhaps we will. I do not believe it will scare us. Perhaps Tori will just be in a playful mood. Then again, it could be quiet.

Everyone wondered how this would play out because of the new understanding we have. It was not as creepy as before. This was different. I wondered if it was because we were growing up as well to add to the case.

The night came when we took the trip to Vampires Grave. We parked our cars in the lot and we got out of the cars. Just being there was a chilling event to witness, however.

Tom asked, "So, are we going in or what?"

I was skeptical. Melissa said, "Sure. Why not?" Melissa walked right in there. I followed and then everyone else came along. We went to the crypt first and chilled there for about ten minutes. Then we went to Tori's headstone.

Tom said, "Troy, I am so sorry about the last time, man. I am so sorry for thinking you were crazy." Tom started to cry.

I put my hand on his shoulder and said, "Hey Tom, it's okay, man. It's all good."

Tom said, "I feel so bad for just seeing this as a horror movie. I never thought about Tori as a person."

I said, "It's all good. I also believe with my heart that Tori forgives you, man. Cheer up."

We all sat in silence for a minute. The atmosphere was different. However, it was also the same. I wondered if Tori was watching us. I did not know what would happen since she told me she was going to rest.

Then we heard footsteps. We were shocked, not knowing what to make of it. Mike said, "Troy are you sure that…"

I interrupted, No it's not Mike. Everyone, Listen, quietly."

Everyone remained quiet and listened. Then we heard a female voice singing. She was singing in another language, and it was beautiful. Then I saw a light and said, "Everyone look. The dancer's platform, mid air!"

Everyone's jaws dropped. We saw Tori dancing and singing on top of the stone, mid air. She was singing in another language as if an opera, yet a new age style song. She had the most gorgeous voice we all ever heard. We were enchanted by the song. Dianna was shaking to her bones. I told her to relax. Melissa was just plain speechless and everyone's eyes were very wide.

I went into my pocket and pulled out my lighter and lit it up as if we were in a concert. Everyone else did the same. We all just stood there, chilled, and listened to the song. After she was done with the song, she looked at all of us, with a smile, and she took a stage bow. We clapped our hands and cheered her on.

Everyone was mesmerized by the enchanted song. Dianna was the first to break out in tears.

Dianna said, "I never expected that. That was so cool."

I said, "I am in awe, everyone."

Everyone agreed. We stayed there and talked about some things for about thirty minutes and then we heard more footsteps. I told everyone to keep calm. It was my friend, Alice.

I introduced Alice to the crew and they were happy to meet her. I thanked Alice for her insights and told her my dream.

I said, "Alice, The great tragedy was, she was forgotten as a person. That is the answer I was looking for."

Alice said, "I know."

I was amazed, "You knew this whole time?"

Alice said "Yes."

I asked, "Why did you not tell me?"

Alice said, "I had to keep the information as you needed to discover it. I figured it out about ten years ago."

I asked, 'Did you see Tori too?"

Alice answered, "Not in the fashion you did. I discovered it in a different way. It's hard to explain."

My other friends were jaw dropped hearing us talk. They were curious about Alice's experience. Tom asked, "Alice, did you get scared here too?"

Alice answered, "Me? Please, hundreds of times. I treated her as a misunderstood vampire once too. Then I realized, when I was twenty years old, that is a person that is buried there. Vampires do not exist."

We all laughed. Mike was just very quiet listening with great intent.

Alice asked, "You all realize that you bear a tale that not many people can say right?"

We never thought of that before. To realize that we have a story that not many people can say was overwhelming. My friends and I gulped.

Alice continued, "This grave is legendary. One of the nation's most haunted places. Think about that."

Again we gulped. I said, "Alice, You are right ma'am.

All of us laughed. Alice stayed with us for about an hour, and she told us how her friends and she were haunted in this cemetery. She brought us to the sites where her crew saw things that creeped the daylights out of them. We had a great time with Alice sharing our memories.

When we parted ways we all returned to Mike's house to have some drinks. We discussed the event that occurred that night. Mike was doing very well.

Mike said, "I tell you all, That was a great song. Can ghosts really sing?

We all said in amazement, "I guess so."

When the night was over we chilled the next day to get ready for the work week. I was not looking forward to work and that was only because there was so much on my mind. As I was going through the week it was Wednesday night and Melissa came over. We chilled for about one hour. She had to go to work due to the need for extra money.

Melissa said, "I am probably going to go to the Community College at this point. I don't know what I will be studying yet."

I said, "Good for you, Melissa."

Melissa continued, "I have an interest in nursing and the health care profession. I do not know what area as of right now."

I said, "Melissa, it's a start."

Melissa asked, "What about you?"

I answered, "I may just stay with mechanics. I like cars. Perhaps I will try college soon."

Melissa said, "The mechanic field is good if you choose to do that. Everyone needs their cars fixed sometimes."

I said, "I know. Plus, I like working on cars. My dad is teaching me brake repair now."

Melissa said, "That's neat. Well, I have to work now, I will see you this weekend."

I said, "See you Melissa. Have a great week."

The next day, I went to see Edna after work and to my surprise, Kenny was there too. We greeted each other with a handshake, as always, Edna made me some coffee.

I asked, Edna? Could Tori sing?"

Edna replied, "Why yes."

Kenny said, "She had an amazing voice. She was part of the school choir and the church choir."

I said, "That is so neat!"

Edna said, She was a lead singer in the church. That was before she got ill."

I went quiet. Every time I thought about Tori getting ill made me sad. I knew it was due to the fact that the illness took her life so young.

Kenny told me, "She loved to sing. Especially in May, as that was her favorite month."

I told them, "I heard her sing at the cemetery the other night,"

Edna said, "Oh?"

Kenny said, "That's amazing. You realize that you witnessed something very rare, right?"

I said, "No, I don't"

Kenny said, "Tori only sings if she likes the person or people. So that is rare."

I almost fell down. I said, "She had an amazing voice."

Kenny said, "I was told she was the best in school and church."

After this, Kenny pulled out a box and he gave me some papers. They were old. He said, "Take this for your memories. These are her diaries. They also speak of her first crush."

I did fall down when I saw this. "Kenny, her own handwriting?"

Kenny said, "Her very own."

I started to cry. "I will cherish these memories forever."

We all talked for about three hours on several different topics. It was a great time and I enjoyed hanging out with them for the time I was there. After we were done I told Edna that I would visit her soon. I returned home and put Tori's diary with my other collection of articles when I was studying her history.

When Saturday approached I learned that Mike's parents were away for the weekend. So the crew decided to crash at Mike's place. We all drank and had a great time. Nobody was driving so we partied pretty hard, still not knowing what will happen to our crew in the days to come. We were trying to make this summer count. We knew a change was going to come. We just did not know when.

We also lit a candle in dedication for Tori and Mike made a sign that said, You Rest In Peace, Tori, Never Forgotten! We all teared up when Mike put it all together.

Mike said, "Well, I guess going to the cemetery will never be the same now."

I said, "Probably not."

Melissa said, "And that is a good thing too."

Dianna agreed saying, "True. We do not need to be going to see a vampire. She was a person. Remembering people that have gone before us can be a wonderful thing."

I said, "Dianna, you just taught me a lesson tonight."

Everyone agreed, shouted, and said, "Cheers," as we held our drinks. Then we played some board games and watched a movie having pizza delivered to the house. The night ended up being one to remember very well.

The next day came and I made another visit to the cemetery by myself. I brought a pizza again, and when I arrived, I said, "Tori, Let's have lunch." As always I ate the whole pizza. I said, "That was a great lunch."

I heard a female voice and this time, I was not scared. She said, "It's such a pretty day today. I would have loved to have been part of your crew."

I turned around and I said, "Tori, You already are, girl, you already are. Forever and ever."

I heard the female voice again. "Forever and ever. It's a great day today."

I said, "It's more than that, Tori, it's an awesome day! I have to return to work now. I will visit again soon"

As I was leaving I saw a female, about nineteen years of age, in a Victorian dress, waiving at me. I smiled and I waived back. I shouted, "Friends! Forever and ever! Then she disappeared. I slowly drove down the road and returned to my house.

As the summer was drawing near to the end, I met up with everyone, and we hung out at the field. We were feeling depressed not knowing about the future. We all pondered what would become of us in the fall.

Dianna said, "I am going to Rhode Island College to study counseling. I want to help people that have been traumatized as I was, when my dad walked out on us."

Melissa said, "I am trying out the nursing program at the Community College."

Tom said, "I am going to Tech school for computers. I am not sure what I will do from there.

Chris said, "Tech school for me, just not sure what yet."

Lori said, "I am going to study paralegal at the Community College. Melissa, I will see you there."

Mike and I were already working on cars. Mike was still bent on staying with the trade and there was no need to go to college. Trade school was a better approach. Mike told us he was going to the tech school for auto repair. I stayed with my dad as he was teaching me cars in his shop.

It was a very hard adjustment for us and I guess that is part of growing up. We all had a tough time with the new adjustments. We just graduated high school and we were new in this working world. I was sad thinking about our departure.

I asked, "Well since none of us are moving out of state, we can all hang out still, right."

Melissa said, "For now. However, we have to face the fact that we could all be separated after life takes us."

We were all depressed when Melissa said that. We knew it was true and no one could deny that. Life is going to take over one day. We just hoped we had a little more time together before that great and dreaded day happened to us.

The rest of the summer was a blast. We tried to make every minute count due to the working world. We did the activities that we always did and one thing was certain. We were not bored. Everyone had a great time with each other for the rest of the summer.

CHAPTER 11

THE FALL AND COLLEGE ARRIVE

Fall has now arrived and my friends were ready for their first day back at college or trade school. Mike and I were the only ones who did not sign up for secondary school yet as we were working in the automotive industry.

Things have changed at this time and we all took notice of it. We could not hang out all together as before. Except for your typical college breaks and summer. Everyone else had different working hours as well. That would also interfere with hanging out as well. Needless-to-say, we were all a little depressed by that, however, we had to adjust.

I was not looking forward to the fall season as always. The longer nights and knowing that winter was ahead always got to me. I was wondering if any of us would make a trip to the cemetery for Halloween at least. I knew we were getting older, however, it would be cool for nostalgia. Even if we saw Tori or not, the trip there would be fun. I would say at least one more time.

To be honest, I have to say that this was a little depressing for me. Life was catching up with us very quickly. I had my thoughts about it. People move, get families, busy at work, yes, life does claim us in due time as it always does.

During these times, we all tried to make an effort to get together, however, all of us at the same time would be a little more rare. Of course this was due to friends having to work evening hours as the company would require. Some of my friends worked on the weekends too. That was also a setback for all of us to get together. Even if we did go to the haunted graveyard, there was a slim chance that it would be all of us.

Mike and I were the only ones who had true day jobs. Working as mechanics we had day time hours and weekends off. It was definitely easy for Mike and I to hang out. The question was, who will make it tonight? Mike and I hung out almost every weekend. We would drink, practice on our guitars, talk jobs, until someone would come along. Yes, things were very different at this time. I could also see it made Mike a little sad too.

Mike said, "Damn, I miss everyone."

I said, "So do I."

Mike said, "I see that you bought a car."

I told Mike, "It's my little beater. I also bought it to fix it up and work on my skills. I am going to rebuild the steering and suspension and the braking system. I am also going to work on the engine to improve performance."

Mike said, "Hey, that is neat."

Mike and I started to hear footsteps and we found that Melissa stopped by. We greeted each other with a hug. Melissa said she was doing well in college so far. We were happy to hear that. I also wondered if anyone else was coming along.

As fate would have it, we were the only ones. We went to Bickfords for dinner and then we went to the field. We talked about several things that mostly pertained to life.

Melissa said, "I miss the younger years when we all could get together."

I said, "I do too. This is sad. I am adjusting though."

Melissa said, "I am too. It still feels weird."

Mike agreed, "It does. I wonder when life will catch up on us totally."

Melissa said, "Don't talk about it. Let's just chill."

During the hangout, we saw that Dianna could make it. She found us at the field and she pulled out some drinks for all of us. We were very happy to see her.

I said, "Dianna, great to see you. I did not think you were coming tonight."

Dianna said, "I had to work a little later, but I am here now."

We all greeted her with a hug and remained at the field for the night. We were having a great time. We started to talk about the memories of Vampire's Grave.

Melissa said, "I miss the whole crew going to the cemetery and getting our wits scared out of us."

Dianna said, "I do too. However, I am glad it's over because we had some horrible times as well."

Melissa said, "That is true. It was still a good time."

I said, "It was, and it is good to know that Tori is a remembered person now."

Mike said, "I'll drink to that. My life is totally back to normal."

Dianna said, "Mine too. Hey, I am doing a killer job in college so far."

I said, "That is awesome."

Dianna replied, My grades are awesome. I never knew that I had it in me."

We were all happy for Dianna. The night ended up turning out very well. We just chilled and talked about possible future plans. We all agreed that all of us were eager to find out what would become of us.

The days moved on and the crew ended up becoming fragmented. We all tried to get together, however, it was becoming more rare. We only ended up hanging out in segments at different times. I have to say that this moment really creeped up on me. I took it the hardest. I am not a fan of goodbyes at all.

Life was moving along and all of my friends were doing well at their schools of choice. We were all busy and trying to save money for apartments and bills. We were very happy that we could all see each other due to where life brought us at this time.

The day came, and to everyone's surprise, all of us got together. What a great moment that was. We decided to take a trip to Vampire's Grave and get a little nostalgia. All of us jumped in our cars and headed off to the cemetery.

When we arrived, we immediately went right into the graveyard without any hesitation. We all knew that Tori would not bother us as in the past. We knew that Tori was still capable of playing a practical joke, however, she would not haunt us. What made the difference was knowing that a person is buried here and not a vampire. Tori was resting in peace as she told me in my dream. This trip was very different for us.

I said, "It's very quiet tonight."

Melissa said, "Yes, but this still produces that awesome nostalgia."

Dianna said, "It sure does."

Tom asked, "I wonder if we will see anything tonight?"

Chris said, "We are older now. Don't get me wrong about the hauntings, however, getting older is making this different."

I knew exactly what Chris was talking about. Don't get me wrong, this was nostalgia, but our age was making things very different. I did not know how to put this in words.

I said, "Well, no matter what, Alice was right. We stand on the ground of one of the most haunted cemeteries of the country. Not many people have a tale that we will have. No matter who believes us, or not."

Everyone agreed and we were thrilled about that fact. To be in the cemetery that even Hollywood would receive inspiration for movies gave us all chills. What a concept it was to behold.

The night had grown a little late and we were all gearing up to leave the cemetery. As we were leaving, we did end up seeing Tori. She was standing by her tombstone waving to all of us. We all waved back at her with a smile on our face. When we left, we decided for a trip to Tommy's for a great burger.

Having everyone on this night was a very special time because it was rare. We tried to make the most of it knowing that we were returning to life on Monday. All of us had a great time and we ended up crashing at my house for nostalgia as well.

Monday came and it was back to the rat race of life. As more time was moving on, I saw my friends doing very well in college. They ended up graduating with their unique plans for their lives ahead.

Melissa moved on and became a nurse. She held her career very successfully at Kent Hospital. She loved helping people and her favorite area was the emergency room.

Chris went on and became a computer installer for construction companies that were building new houses and office buildings. He was the manager for the company he was working for.

Lori ended up opening her own pizza shop. She was successful and her pizzeria was completely awesome. She was so good at it that Rhode Island voted her "Rhode Island's Best!" Every time I went to her pizzeria, I always got my food free of charge.

Tom became a computer software engineer having received a Bachelor Degree in computer science. He had a very well paying job in the state of Massachusetts. Tom also ended up moving to Attleboro and we would see him about six times a year.

Dianna received her Masters Degree and got a job in counseling for troubled teens. As Dianna had life experience as a troubled teen, and with her degree, she was one of the most consulted counselors that was sought out. She did a very good job in what she was doing with her profession.

Mike stayed as an automotive technician. He was working for a well known company in Rhode Island as a lead diagnostic technician. Mike was a very good mechanic and many people sought him out for work on their vehicles.

I was the same as Mike, becoming an automotive technician. My specialty was steering and suspension systems. I had a very good job at a company in Rhode Island and I was sought out for those who had steering and suspension issues with their vehicles.

As far as Vampire's Grave is concerned, I became like Edna and visited the site once or twice a year. Every time I went, I brought a small pizza and a guitar pick. I would eat the whole pizza and then I would place the guitar pick at Tori's headstone. Every time I made a visit I heard a female voice saying, "It's a very pretty day today. I am perfectly ok today." I would reply back saying, "Today is an excellent day. That was a great lunch."

It is a privilege having the great friends that I did. It was remarkable that we stood on the ground of Rhode Island's most notorious cemetery many times. The thoughts that arrive in my mind; about legends, Hollywood, books, and the likes, always give me chills to my very bones. My friends and I carry a story that not many people can tell, whether they believe us or not.

Be very careful, however, should you ever visit the haunted grave for yourself. The cemetery is not a joke, and the legend is chilling. Beware the ghost that haunts the grave. Beware the footsteps that you might make. For on the site that you will stand, Tori's ghost may be at hand. Rest In Peace Tori! Always Remembered!

About The Author:

Troy A. Lembicz

Troy A. Lembicz is a professional Automotive Technician with fifteen years of experience. Having a true dedication to the automotive industry he has a great reputation among the business world and customer satisfaction.

Troy is also a musician who can play guitar, drums, and keyboards. He has a sole interest in writing his own music in a few different genres. Music has been a true passion for Troy his whole life and he is inspired by music when creating a fictional tale.

Troy has a fascination with adventure and lore stories in both forms of books and movies. This fascination combined with music inspired him to write out Vampire's Grave, A Rhode Island Story. Troy's favorite genres are adventure, lore, romance, drama, sci-fi, and action. This gave him the necessary motivation to write the fictional story.

Author Contact:

thetrasiantale17@gmail.com